The Quetzal Feather

Also by Frances Riker Duncombe:

CASSIE'S VILLAGE

The QUETZAL FEATHER

Frances Riker Duncombe

DRAWINGS AND MAP BY
W. T. Mars

Lothrop, Lee & Shepard Co., Inc.
NEW YORK

acknowledgment

So MANY PEOPLE HELPED ME IN THE COLLECTING OF material and also in the writing of *The Quetzal Feather* that to name each one just wouldn't be possible. To all, I give most grateful thanks. One person, though, I shall name. It was because of her that I wanted to write this book.

At the time of her death, Jane Winton Gottlieb and I were collaborating on an adult novel about Alvarado's conquest of Guatemala and the twenty years that followed it. The choice of subject and the initial enthusiasm were hers. That book I found I couldn't finish without her, but much of the research we did for it together has gone into this book. And from the unfinished adult novel I took Luis, Demonio, and Echeverria.

F.R.D.

foreword

SOME PEOPLE LIKE TO KNOW NOT ONLY WHAT HAPPENS but why . . . and what happens afterward. For these people, I have put at the back of the book a few pages telling of what led to the conquest of Guatemala and some of the things that happened after *The Quetzal Feather* ends.

To make the geography of the story less confusing, I have referred to all land known as Guatemala at the end of the Conquest by that name. In reality only Cakchiquel territory, and perhaps only their capital city Iximché and the land right around it, was meant when Alvarado spoke of Guatemala in 1524.

Names of Indian people and places are spelled in many different ways by those who wrote of the Conquest at the time, and also by those who wrote of it later. Where versions differ, I have chosen the most familiar spelling and, where none is likely to be familiar to the reader, that which is easiest to pronounce.

Luis, Bartolomé, Tzián, Rojas, and Echeverria are fictional characters. So are the horses—Demonio, Mamacita, and Preciosa. All other characters named in *The Quetzal Feather* were actual members of Alvarado's expedition or Indians of the towns and cities he conquered.

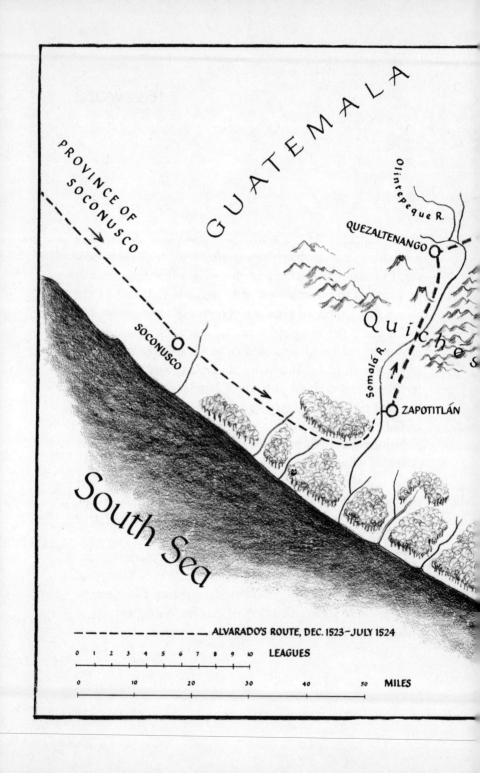

GUATEMALA

PROVINCE OF SOCONUSCO

Olintepeque R.

QUEZALTENANGO

Quichés

SOCONUSCO

Somalá R.

ZAPOTITLÁN

South Sea

– – – – ALVARADO'S ROUTE, DEC. 1523–JULY 1524

0 1 2 3 4 5 6 7 8 9 10   LEAGUES

0   10   20   30   40   50   MILES

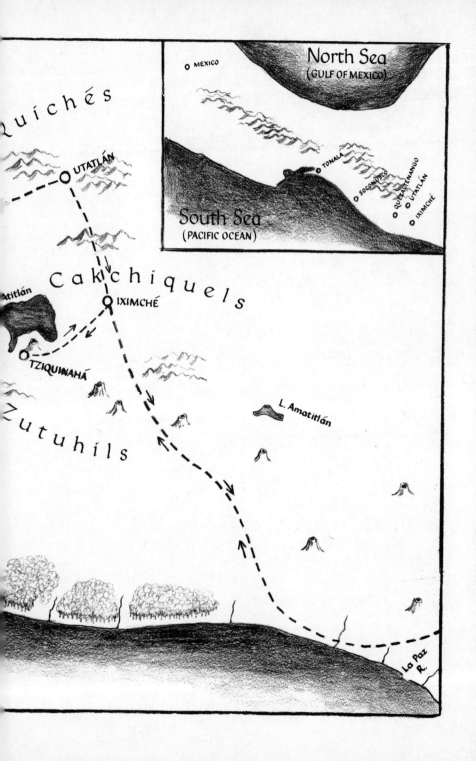

Quichés

UTATLÁN

Cakchiquels

Atitlán

IXIMCHÉ

TZIQUINAHÁ

Zutuhils

North Sea
(GULF OF MEXICO)

○ MEXICO

South Sea
(PACIFIC OCEAN)

○ TONALA

SOCONUSCO

QUEZALTENANGO

UTATLÁN

IXIMCHÉ

L. Amatitlán

La Paz
R.

THE ARMY, AS USUAL WHILE ON THE MARCH, HAD MADE camp early so the horses could eat and drink their fill before morning. Watched over by Indian attendants, more than a hundred and fifty animals were cropping dry, brownish grass on the plain and drinking in the stream that trickled through it. They belonged to the expedition of Pedro de Alvarado, sent south from Mexico by Cortés in December of 1523 to gain new lands and subjects for Spain in far-off Guatemala. Now, early in February, the expedition was passing through the province of Soconusco, just north of the country it had come to conquer.

The only horses not already grazing in the late afternoon sunlight were those waiting to be shod at the forge on the outskirts of camp. One of these, a young black stallion, was held by a boy of fourteen in ragged cotton clothing. The horse was named Demonio and the boy called himself Luis López.

Luis scuffed his dusty boots in the trampled ground that circled the forge and thought what he could say when it came Demonio's turn to be shod. The horse had cast a shoe that morning and though Luis had searched he hadn't been able to find it. New shoes were becoming scarce and every day they grew more dear. Luis had no money at all, so the problem was acute.

The blacksmith pounded a final nail into the hoof of a sorrel mare and nodded to Luis. "You next, *chico*."

"I have no money," Luis stammered, "but—"

Without waiting for him to finish the sentence, for which as yet he'd thought of no ending, the smith beckoned to a man holding a rough-coated bay.

Luis gulped. Before the man moved forward to the forge, he must find a way to soften the blacksmith's heart. An idea came.

"But, *señor*, how can you say No when Demonio asks you so politely?" He touched the horse under the right foreleg and the animal stretched out both front legs and lowered his head over them as though bowing to the smith.

The men gathered around the forge laughed in appreciation of the horse's trick. "*Por Dios*, the animal did not learn such manners from Echeverria," one remarked, slapping at an insect crawling on his leathery neck.

"He did not," Luis replied. "It was I who taught him. From Captain Echeverria he learned nothing but to kick and rear and defend himself against cruelty. But for me, as you can see, he is like a lamb."

Beneath his tangle of curling dark hair, the boy's face flushed in boastful pride. Then his expression became one of pleading. "With only three shoes Demonio will go lame on the march tomorrow. As you know, the ground is

baked hard as brick, *Por favor*, Señor Sánchez, do not refuse him a shoe."

Diego Sánchez was a huge burly man who looked like
a brigand, but his hands were gentle as he lifted and
examined the horse's near front hoof. Its walls were badly
chipped.

"So the animal belongs to Captain Echeverria," he said.
"Why didn't you say so, boy? I have no love for the man
but if he fails to pay me in pesos, I can always take iron
instead. His Negro slaves, poor unfortunates, carry enough
iron bars on their backs to make a thousand horseshoes."

Luis hesitated, tempted to let the matter go at that; let
Sánchez shoe the horse on Echeverria's credit. Then he
knew he couldn't. It would be one more sin on his soul
until he dared confess to Father Godinez. The sins, though
small, were mounting so rapidly that if each had been a
pebble, already there would be enough to fill two boots.

He lifted his head resolutely. "No, the horse is mine. It
is I who will pay somehow. I, Luis—" Suddenly he caught
his lip between his teeth. "I, Luis López." The last name
came out in a voice too loud. Almost, almost he had forgotten and used the name to which he had been born. A
name which Pedro Alvarado, who led the expedition,
would surely recognize if he heard it repeated.

"The boy is right." The man holding the bay horse
nodded. "The day after Echeverria won the black at dice,
he gave him to the boy. I was there." He chuckled. "It
was two weeks ago when the Soconuscans rose against us
at Tonalá. The animal had unseated Echeverria three times.
When he mounted the fourth time, it reared over back-

ward, almost crushing him. After the horse ran off he vowed he wanted no more of the brute except for saddle and bridle. He offered him to anyone who could catch him and bring those back. The boy did."

It was an accurate enough account of the transaction, Luis agreed. That is, if one left out all the anger and cruelty. He, Luis, could not. As though it were all happening over again right now, hot blood rushed to his head. His heart pounded and his throat grew dry and scratchy.

Again, he was on the plains of Tonalá. The battle was over and the enemy fleeing in wild disorder from the horses. Never having seen the animals before, they took them for angry and powerful gods. Those in the rear had come up, and Luis was watching the pursuing cavalry disappear into the distance when a harsh voice called out to him.

"Boy, hold this brute's head."

It was Echeverria, an infantry officer. He was off his horse and having difficulty in remounting. Every time he tried, the animal swung away from him. Luis grasped the reins close to the bit and the Captain gained the saddle. Before Luis had time to loosen his hold, he felt the reins jerk.

"Stand back, you fool!"

At the same instant, Echeverria was sawing at the horse's mouth and digging the rowels of his spurs into his sides. Luis only had time to see the pain in the animal's eyes and the nostrils flaring wide in fright when the front legs rose and hoofs brushed against his shoulder. He jumped aside before they came down again. The horse

reared a second time. And why not? Luis thought. Afraid to go forward against the cruel bit and raked by the spurs in his sides, the animal had only one defense. Up, up, he went. At the height of his rear, the flat of Echeverria's sword came down between his ears with the sickening sound of metal against bone.

Again and again the horse reared. His mouth was bleeding cruelly now. Blood ran down between his eyes, and blood and froth spattered his black chest and sides. Each time he reared the sword came down on his head, but each time he rose again.

"Don't, don't," Luis cried but no one heard him. Certainly not Echeverria who was cursing loudly.

Then it happened. Reaching for the sky with his front feet, the horse teetered. For a moment that seemed long, Luis watched. The ugly scar on Echeverria's cheek was as red as the horse's blood, his eyes as merciless as the steel of the sword he was bringing down once more on the animal's head. As it descended, the horse screamed and threw himself over backward. Echeverria rolled clear. The horse rolled too and then was up again, galloping off riderless with stirrups flapping against his sides.

The moon was high above the plains when Luis next saw the horse. For an hour or more he wouldn't let Luis come up with him. He did not run but always he moved just out of reach, listening to Luis' voice but ready to wheel and run if any sudden move were made. Luis had all but given up when the horse allowed him to come close and stroke his neck. It was sunrise when he led him back to camp and delivered saddle and bridle to Echeverria, claiming his reward.

"Keep him and be damned!" Echeverria had roared. "The brute is well named 'Demonio.' He will kill you the first time you climb on his back." Several officers were standing near at the time; among them Don Pedro Puerto-carrero, one of Alvarado's most respected captains of cavalry.

For several days Luis had made no attempt to ride Demonio. During the marches he led him well to the rear of the column with the relay horses, as the extra animals taken along were called. Sometimes he led another horse also, a placid brown and white mare named Mamacita, who had a quieting effect on every horse with whom she traveled. At other times Bartolomé, a young Tlascalan Indian of Luis' own age, was given Mamacita to lead. Then Luis would walk close to him so the two horses could be together. And always he spoke softly to Demonio as he had to Peciosa, the little chestnut filly he'd once owned in Spain.

When one evening Luis mounted Demonio for the first time, bareback and with only a halter and rope woven of henequen fiber for bridle and reins, he fully expected the horse to rear and throw him. But Demonio had stood quite still. When Luis tightened his legs and put spurless heels to Demonio's sides, the animal moved out quietly, head carried free on his long graceful neck. Not once since then had he been unruly. He was a mount any man could be proud of. More, he was a friend. That he should go lame for lack of a shoe was unthinkable.

"Please, Señor Sánchez," Luis pleaded once more,

"Until I can pay, I shall help you at the forge whenever you ask. And until he is needed in battle, Demonio will carry my weight in nails for you every day."

"One shoe, then," the smith grunted, setting down the hoof. "You can start right now at the bellows."

"May the good St. Francis bless you," Luis said gratefully.

As Sánchez shaped the shoe and fitted it against the hoof, one of the soldiers watching the operation gave Luis a piece of friendly advice. "In your place, young one, I would not let it appear that the horse is so gentle now. I have seen Echeverria eyeing him several times lately when he comes to the rear to inspect his slaves. Suppose he changes his mind and wants him back?"

"If he does, I shall refuse," Luis replied. "Don Pedro Puertocarrero would support me. He was witness to the gift."

"Well, that is to the good." The man scratched himself.

"But what about Gonzalo Alvarado, our Captain's brother?" another soldier asked. "He is a crony of Echeverria's and would side with him. He might take the matter to His Excellency."

"If he should, I know His Excellency would uphold my rights." In all of New Spain there was no one, in Luis' eyes, who could compare with the handsome and smiling blond conquistador whom the Tlascalans had nicknamed "Tonatiuh," meaning "The Sun." Every since Luis had first seen him, on coming to Mexico three months before, he'd been as drawn to Alvarado as though he really were the sun. It was why he had had to follow him.

"Your rights, young one?" The man laughed. "You haven't been long in this army or you wouldn't talk of rights."

Luis glared at him but actually he was more worried than he cared to show and his worry had to do with the horse. Not, though, for the reason the man had insinuated. Not for a moment did Luis doubt the honor and fairness of Alvarado. No, there was a different reason for his worry.

He was not inscribed on the army rolls; neither under the name of López nor under his real name. He had, in fact, joined the army in a manner somewhat lacking in formality. So far Alvarado hadn't noticed him but if Echeverria complained about Demonio, it would bring him to the Captain's attention. Questions would be asked— questions Luis didn't want to answer. At least, not for a while longer. As the whole camp knew, before they left the province of Soconusco messengers would set out for Mexico bearing Alvarado's report to the Captain-General Cortés. Luis did not wish to be sent back to Mexico with them. When they had gone he would be safe. No one would send a boy alone on such a long and difficult journey.

Ahead lay the road to adventure and incredible riches, if one could believe the stories. The Indians of the land they had come to conquer were said to be the richest in the whole New World. Gold was reported to be so plentiful that it was used for axes and other ordinary purposes; jeweled ornaments were reported of greater splendor than those taken from Montezuma in Mexico. There would be glory too. Once they left Soconusco and there was no longer need to avoid attention, he and Demonio would distinguish themselves in battle against hordes of infidel savages. Alvarado would single them out for praise.

No, most decidedly, Luis did not wish to be sent back with the messengers. He pumped the bellows faster, and the wood in the forge glowed and sparked.

chapter

꒜꒜꒜꒜꒜꒜꒜꒜

2

EXCEPT FOR MINOR SKIRMISHES AND THE BATTLE OF Tonalá, there had been no fighting in the two months of hot dusty marching that the army had been on the road. After Tonalá, all resistance to the army's progress southward had ceased. The march continued along the coastal plains of the subdued province of Soconusco, and the few small thatch-roofed villages along the way met the conquistadores with food, not arrows.

Either in the lead or at the head of the infantry, Alvarado rode his big chestnut gelding, the only animal in the whole outfit that Luis felt could compare with Demonio. Sometimes Don Pedro Puertocarrero or another officer rode at Alvarado's side; sometimes it was his Indian wife, the beautiful Tlascalan princess, Doña Luisa, who rode beside him on her gray mule. Over narrow roads, beaten hard by generations of Indian travel, the army moved in a long column: a hundred and thirty-five horsemen, three hundred Spanish foot soldiers, and four hundred Mexican and Tlascalan warriors—loyal allies of

Spain. Besides the fighting men there were other Spaniards and many other Indians, both men and women.

When the army had left Mexico, escorted for the first
hour by the Captain-General Cortés, it had presented a
dazzling spectacle. Pennons had waved in the cool breeze
that rippled the gaudy feathered headdresses of the chieftains. Sun glinted on the helmets of cavalry and infantry;
on the shining tips of spears, and the four small brass cannon. It shone on the large crucifix carried in front of the
priests and the Franciscan friars who accompanied the expedition and on the rich velvets of the representatives of
the Crown.

Now, because of the heat, full armor was no longer
worn, even by those who owned it, and dust from the road
dimmed the shine of metal and lay like powder on velvet
and feathers.

Each group had its own position in the line of march.
Directly ahead of the rear guard and behind the baggage
were the relay horses. Luis had chosen a position for himself among them even before he'd owned Demonio.
Though his heart was always ahead, physically he wished
to be as far removed from Alvarado as possible. He made
himself useful and attracted no particular attention.

As the column made its way forward under a sun that
grew continually hotter, Luis found himself glad of Bartolomé's company. The young Tlascalan was the only
attendant traveling with the relay animals to whom he
could make himself understood.

"You speak Spanish well, Bartolomé. Quite like a
Spaniard," he had complimented him one afternoon early

in the campaign when they were leading their horses side by side. The march had begun at dawn and occasionally Luis stumbled, but Bartolomé's stocky bronze body still moved in effortless rhythm, half walk, half trot.

"*Gracias*, Luis, but it is nothing," he replied with a shrug. "I speak the Mexican language also."

"You were in Mexico long?" Luis asked.

"Four years. I came from Tlascala with Tia Luisa when she married Tonatiuh."

"Doña Luisa! She's your aunt?" He had thought Bartolomé as much alone as himself.

"*Seguro*. Her father, the blind king of Tlascala, was my grandfather."

Luis stared in astonishment. "Then why are you here among the horses, Bartolomé, instead of ahead with the chieftains?"

Beyond the baggage carriers and the warriors, the feathered headdresses of the chieftains made a splash of color against the dry burned landscape. Bartolomé's eyes went forward to the plumes and then returned to Luis.

"And why should I be ahead any more than you?" he asked. "The clothes you wear do not hide that you, too, are highly born."

The remark worried Luis. Suppose Bartolomé talked to Doña Luisa about a highly born Spanish boy among the Indian attendants? This mustn't happen. Yet Bartolomé was too intelligent to deceive about his birth.

"You are right in thinking I am well born, Bartolomé," he said slowly. "But I hoped that fact was better hidden. I have an uncle, my father's brother. He beat me. I ran away. I don't want anyone to know I am with the army. Not until it is too late to send me back."

All of this was true, but the picture it painted was not true. Tio Rodrigo had beaten him too often after his father's death, certainly. But it wasn't from Tio Rodrigo that Luis had run away. His uncle was in Spain, in the province of Estremadura. The house from which Luis had run away was a palace in Mexico.

Before he died the year before, Luis' father had made all the arrangements for him to come to Mexico. Tio Rodrigo hadn't approved of the plan but neither had he forbidden it when the time for sailing came. He had only talked of the risk of such a journey and how stories of wealth in the New World were exaggerated. Tio Rodrigo had a fear of danger and adventure and no more love for spirit in boys than in horses; he used the whip too much on both. Luis' mother liked Tio Rodrigo. Luis did not, but if mention of his beatings gained Bartolomé's sympathy and silence, Luis resolved to pray for his uncle as well as for his mother that night.

Bartolomé's expression was hard to read. Luis wondered if he'd made a mistake, after all, in speaking as he had. Then without his expression changing, Bartolomé said in a voice filled with hatred, "I, too, have an uncle who tried to prevent me from following Tonatiuh. He conspired against the Spaniards, though the king had made peace."

"Then you won't say anything of what I've told you?"

"No, Luis. I will not. Until you tell me it is safe to do so."

Bartolomé had kept his word and league by league the distance between Luis and safety shortened.

The next to last night they made camp in the province of Soconusco, Luis found it hard to sleep, though the march had been a long one and his legs felt as heavy as the sack of nails that Demonio carried every day for the blacksmith. It was partly excitement that the danger of discovery was nearly over and partly the mosquitoes. They feasted on every uncovered portion of his body and slap as he would, he couldn't drive them away. The mosquitoes were bothering the horses also. Luis could tell by the way they stamped their feet and swished their tails.

Well, if sleep wouldn't come, there was plenty to think about; things to do with the campaign that he'd heard discussed around the forge by Diego Sánchez and some of the soldiers. In Guatemala, it seemed, there were many kingdoms of Indians, each ruled over by two kings jointly. The strongest of these were the Quichés, the Cakchiquels, and the Zutuhils, all of whom had their capitals in the high lands beyond a formidable range of mountains. It was said the priests and friars counted on converting thousands of these savages and establishing small colonies among them where the teaching of the True Faith could be continued.

Luis agreed that the winning of so many souls for God would be a fine thing but he hoped the winning wouldn't be too easy. First there must be some hard-fought battles in which he could ride Demonio.

There was also talk of searching for a strait between the North and South seas, through which Spanish ships could sail to the Isles of Spice. If Alvarado could discover such a strait, he would gain great favor in Spain. So everyone said.

Luis turned restlessly from his stomach to his back and looked up at the dark blot that was Demonio, tethered beside him. The horse raised his head and seemed to be listening; then he went back to grazing. Luis returned to his thoughts. When they met the Quichés it wouldn't be for the first time. These people had sent a small army to help the Soconuscans at Tonalá, hoping to wipe out the expedition before it set foot on Quiché soil. Several of their chieftains had been captured in battle. Alvarado had treated them kindly and sent them as messengers to their kings, offering friendship to the Quiché people if they would give allegiance to Carlos V, King of Spain. He had also asked for safe passage through their country. Luis thought of these chieftains with anger. They had taken Alvarado's gifts, promising to return with replies. They had not returned.

On the ground beside Luis lay Bartolomé, breathing evenly as though in sleep. Then his breath stopped. He was awake, Luis realized, and listening to something. He held his own breath. Quite near them was a sound that neither boy might have heard if the horses hadn't been still at that moment. It was no louder than the whisper of grass bending. Then Demonio nickered softly as a mare tethered on the opposite side of the thorn bush moved to the end of her rope. The mare was Mamacita and she didn't respond to Demonio's nicker except to stop. When she moved again her hoof struck against a stone and a spark shone briefly in the darkness.

Mamacita was restless because of the heat and insects and because she was in foal, Luis decided. He had raised himself on one elbow, the better to listen. Now he lay down and closed his eyes again. Immediately, though, his eyelids flew open. The spark, it had been too far away. Beyond a rope's length. The mare must have pulled loose. She would have to be caught before she wandered off.

Luis scrambled to his feet. "Bartolomé, Mamacita is loose. We must catch her." He put a hand down to shake the boy, but Bartolomé had already risen and was standing quietly beside him.

There was only a sliver of moon, thin as the edge of a fingernail. The ground was black and the horses were black too. Only those that stood between the boys and the moon could be distinguished at all, dark silhouettes against a slightly less dark background.

Bartolomé said a few words in Tlascalan to a man on the ground and then followed Luis.

The mare had been tethered at the edge of the pasture and there were neither attendants nor other horses between her and the open plains. She was not hurrying toward freedom, though. The soft clop-clop of her hoofs was the sound of walking. She was only fifty or sixty feet ahead and Luis knew they could come up with her easily if she were not startled into running. He moved to the right of her heels and sent Bartolomé to the left. Silently, or so Luis thought, they began to close in on her.

The mare quickened her pace, taking up a slow jog. They were a couple of hundred yards from the other horses now but Luis wasn't worried. Mamacita was lazy. She would soon walk again. In the meantime it wasn't hard to keep up with her. The only difficulty lay in avoiding bushes and holes in the darkness.

A few minutes later the mare did stop. At almost the same instant Luis ran against a low-growing cactus and sprawled on his face. Above him something swift passed, stirring the air. He heard it whistle through space and then rattle in the branches of a bush. An arrow! Luis knew the sound but he couldn't quite believe his ears. Instinctively, though, he rolled several times before getting up. Another arrow came, burying itself in the ground he had just quit.

"*Aquí*, Luis," Bartolomé called. "Come quickly!"

Ahead there was scuffling and snorting and grunting. Luis rushed forward and became entangled in flailing legs and arms. There was a rope too—Mamacita's halter rope. He caught hold of it and was lifted high into the air. When he came down, his feet struck into a naked belly, round and hard like a ball, but slippery like butter. It collapsed under his weight and breath rushed out in a long sigh. Luis felt cold in his own stomach and as though he might be sick. He didn't know whether it was friend or enemy on whom he'd landed. All he really knew was that he was still clinging to the rope tied to Mamacita's halter and it was burning his fingers as she tried to pull away.

"The rope, Luis! You have knocked out his breath. Give me the rope quickly so I can bind him."

Praise be to the Blessed Virgin, the voice was Bartolomé's. Luis stepped back from the motionless body and untied the rope, holding tight to the halter at the same time. His fingers were clumsy because he was shaking all over. Bartolomé took the rope and, stooping over, wound it around the man on the ground.

"Dog! Thief!" he spat down at him. "If I hadn't lost my knife, I'd cut out your heart for sacrifice!"

Luis couldn't see Bartolomé's face but the fierceness in his voice brought out prickles on his skin. Would Bartolomé really have cut out the heart of their prisoner? Luis didn't know. It was impossible for him to feel certain about anything with Indians—even those who seemed civilized like Bartolomé. Perhaps he had known all along that the mare was being stolen.

Luis felt himself growing angry. "You let me be shot at rather than warn me of the man," he accused Bartolomé. "You wanted him to lead us beyond the hearing of the others so you could cut out his heart."

"No, no, I did not." All the fierceness was gone from Bartolomé's voice. It was stiff and hurt. "Only when I heard the arrow fly did I know anyone was near Mamacita. Except for her hoofs, yours were the only feet I heard. If you will pardon me, Luis, you made as much noise as an army. And as for what I said, it was to frighten the man only. You should remember I am a Christian. I know as well as you that our Lord does not permit human sacrifice."

So. Luis was glad he'd been mistaken. He was sorry he had hurt Bartolomé's pride.

"Forgive me, Bartolomé," he said. "And I am sorry about the noise. All the time I thought I was making no sound at all. I wish I could walk as silently as you."

"If you like, I will be your teacher," Bartolomé offered, willing to forget the quarrel.

At their feet the prisoner grunted.

"We must get him back to camp," Luis said. "Mamacita will have to carry him."

Together the boys hoisted the man across the back of the docile mare, his head hanging down on one side and his feet on the other. He had regained his breath and was complaining loudly in guttural tones. Neither of the boys understood his language and neither cared whether he was comfortable or not. When he was safely disposed, Bartolomé picked up the bow and quiver and then waited for Luis to lead the way. Leadership belonged to the Spaniard. Both boys knew this.

Luis set out bravely, but before he had taken more than a few steps he was sure they were in the wrong direction. He stopped and peered into the darkness on all sides but he could see nothing.

"Do you know where we are, Bartolomé?"

"*Sí,* I know."

"Then walk at the horse's head and I will guard the prisoner." It was an order. It preserved dignity.

The prisoner lay still across Mamacita's back but he kept up a steady flow of words. Were they some Soconuscan dialect, Luis wondered? Or Quiché perhaps?

Walking beside the man, for the first time since the capture Luis had opportunity to think calmly of how near he'd come to death at the hands of this stranger. If he hadn't stumbled at the exact moment, the first arrow would have found him. He would not now be walking at the side of Mamacita, bringing a prisoner back to the camp. When the sun rose tomorrow he would not have seen it; when the column moved out in the morning some-

one else would have led Demonio. Not even once would
he have ridden him in battle. No one would have known
the true name of the boy who had died. His mother could
not have been told so that candles might be lit in his name.

These were sobering thoughts. Lost in them, Luis wasn't
conscious of how far they'd walked.

"Halt!" A loud voice came suddenly out of the darkness. Then a lantern was unshielded and glared in his eyes.

Mamacita halted so suddenly that her burden slipped
to the ground at the feet of a sentry guarding a shelter
made of branches. He turned his light on the squirming,
cursing figure and then back on the boys.

"Who is this man, trussed like a pig for roasting?" he
asked.

"A thief," Luis said, feeling a sudden belated pride in
what surely had been a great achievement.

The sentry laughed mockingly. "Not a likely story,
chico. You should think of a better one. Is it not rather
a prank you have played on one of our allies? And the
horse? To whom does it belong and how dared you take
it? Well, you two young ones have much to explain to the
Captain of the Guards."

He called another sentry and then, grasping Luis and
Bartolomé each by an arm, he started to march them away.

"It was not a prank! The man isn't an ally. He was stealing the mare and we made him our prisoner," Luis shouted,
trying to pull away.

"Do you take me for a fool?" The sentry's voice rose
high in anger. "The natives of this country fear horses
as we fear the devil."

The henequen cloth at the entrance of the shelter was drawn back and a man came out. It was Alvarado. Dressed only in a rumpled shirt, he looked sleepy and ill-humored.

"What's the meaning of this infernal racket?" he roared. "After working half the night a man needs sleep, not a hullabaloo outside his quarters!"

Luis turned his face toward the sentry, his heart thumping hard. "I will come, *señor*," he said in a low voice. "Let us go quickly."

But now the sentry began to explain. He shone his lantern first on Mamacita, then on the figure on the ground, and then on the two boys. "A prank, Excellency," he said. "These boys shall be well punished. It appears they have helped themselves to a horse and trussed up its attendant."

"Wait." Alvarado leaned forward and looked hard at the boys. "This one I know," he said, nodding toward Bartolomé. "He is the nephew of Doña Luisa. The face of the other is also familiar, though I can't place it. I will question the boys myself."

Luis felt as though his feet were growing into the ground like the roots of a tree. Even if escape had been possible, he couldn't have moved. So, after all, he would be sent back to Mexico with the messengers when they left.

"What is your name, boy? And what are you doing with this horse?" The questions were directed at Luis and the voice was stern. Luis swallowed but no words came.

"Well, speak up." The voice was impatient now. "And let it be the truth. Or shall I ask Bartolomé?"

Luis took a deep breath and straightened his shoulders. He looked straight into the angry blue eyes boring into his.

"I will speak for myself, Excellency, and it will be the truth."

chapter

〓〓〓〓〓〓〓〓

3

THE MOMENT THAT LUIS HAD BEEN FEARING FOR TWO months confronted him. And it had come not through Echeverria, as he had expected, but through an act of courage on his own part. It was not just of fate to have brought him to Alvarado's attention for such a reason, he felt, especially when safety lay no more than a day or so ahead.

Luis stood straight as a lance and his eyes never left Alvarado's. The Captain would send him back to Mexico. He would have to. Not only discipline but loyalty to Cortés demanded it. Luis knew his respect and admiration for the great Captain would suffer if he acted otherwise, but that was cold comfort. In every corner of his heart and every sinew of his body, desire to follow Alvarado was an overwhelming urge. In spite of himself his lower lip shot out childishly.

Behind him, Mamacita was munching on a tuft of dry grass. On the ground the trussed Indian grunted. From the far side of the pasture where the horses were picketed came the hoot of an owl. Inside the shelter someone was moving about.

The muscles of Luis' stomach sucked in until they seemed to touch his spine as he began to speak.

"Excellency, the horse is a relay animal . . ."

"Whoo, whooo." The owl's hoot had an insistent, questioning note.

"Her name is Mamacita . . ."

"Whoo, whooo."

"Listen, O Tonatiuh," Bartolomé broke in, stepping forward.

Luis saw anger flare in Alvarado's eyes and his hand lift as though to strike the boy, but the young Indian went on fearlessly.

"Listen to the owl, Tonatiuh. He is not speaking owl language."

Alvarado's raised hand drew back and went to his ear, cupping it.

"Whoo, whooo." Again the sound came. Everyone was listening now except the prisoner whose voice suddenly rose in loud howls.

"Silence the man," Alvarado ordered curtly.

Once more the owl hooted.

"Morales, take extra guards to the pasture and see that the attendants are awake." Alvarado snapped out the command. "Bartolomé is right. That is no owl."

One of the sentries disappeared from the circle of lantern light. Luis turned to watch him go. With the glare of the lanterns no longer in his eyes, he could see the blackness of night was lifting. The stars were pale in a dark gray sky.

"Now I will hear what you have to say, boy." Alvarado's attention returned to Luis. "You have been accused of playing a prank on one of our allies charged with watching over the horses. Is this true?"

"No, Excellency. It is not true." Luis spoke boldly, feeling a great surge of relief. This was not a question he feared answering. "The mare was in my care. The man was stealing her. Bartolomé and I captured him."

"It is so, Tonatiuh," Bartolomé corroborated. "The dog is not one of the allies; he comes from an enemy tribe. He shot twice at Luis. This is his bow and these are his arrows." He held bow and quiver out to Alvarado.

Alvarado examined them closely. "Quiché," he grunted. "Let an interpreter be sent for. In the meantime loosen the man's bonds so he may stand, but keep close guard over him."

As one of the guards stooped to obey, Alvarado turned toward the shelter.

"Have I Your Excellency's permission to return to my duty?" Luis asked hopefully.

"Not yet." Alvarado drew back the henequen curtain of the shelter and stepped inside. A murmur of voices came to Luis' ears—one deep and one soft and gentle.

"Tonatiuh consults with Tia Luisa," Bartolomé informed him. "She is telling him to trust our story no matter what the dog says."

When the interpreter arrived, Alvarado emerged from the shelter fully clothed and carrying a whip of braided leather. "Ask the prisoner from what place he comes and who sent him to steal the mare," he commanded.

The interpreter, a small wizened old man who had once

been a slave at the Quiché court, glared at the captive with hatred as he put the question. There was an exchange of unintelligible sounds and then the interpreter translated.

"He says he was not stealing the mare. He was but leading her to water because she was thirsty."

Alvarado gave a short laugh. "Try again. Tell him that Tonatiuh can be kind but that he can also be severe."

Again there was a garbled exchange of sounds. "The dog insists it is as he said," the interpreter reported.

"Some lashes and he may be willing to speak the truth." Alvarado gave the order amiably, handing his whip to one of the soldiers who had gathered around.

When the lash came down for the first time, Luis felt excitement and a savage sense of pleasure. The man had tried to kill him; he deserved pain.

The whip came down for the second time and the captive howled in agony. A third and a fourth lash. The man's back was streaming with blood now.

When the whip cracked a fifth time, Luis looked away.

"Enough." Alvarado's voice was still amiable. "Put the question again."

This time the prisoner spoke so volubly that the interpreter had a hard time keeping up with him. He was from the Quiché capital, Gumarcaah, called Utatlán by the Mexicans. He had been ordered by the kings to steal a horse and bring it back so their people could see that these strange animals were not gods against whom it was useless to fight. He had followed the march for over a week, studying the animals. He had chosen the most placid one.

"Well, now we have part of the truth," Alvarado said in satisfaction. "Ask him about his companion, the one who speaks like an owl."

"He says he was alone," the interpreter translated after asking the question. "He knows nothing about any owl."

Alvarado nodded to the soldier with the whip. As he

stepped forward the man threw back his head and from his throat came the scream of a night hawk, shrill and piercing. It was still ringing in the air when the lash came down. The Quiché fell to the ground.

"He will talk," the interpreter said, bending over and listening to the hoarse whisper. "His companion was Prince Ahzumanche, one of the kings' favorite warriors. He says you will never catch him now that he has given the warning."

"We will meet in battle, though," Alvarado said grimly. "The kings would not seek to acquaint their people with the horse unless they intended to fight us."

He put out his hand for the whip. "No more need of that. Brand the man as a slave taken in war and give him a load to carry on the march."

With a yawn he turned away. Pink streaks were beginning to show in the sky. "I can still get an hour's sleep," he said. "This morning we do not march but review the troops. Tomorrow we enter Guatemala and by the looks of things the Quichés will not wait to receive us in their capital. We can expect attack any time after we cross the border."

Luis stared at the ground. He didn't dare look up for fear someone would notice the relief in his eyes. It was a reprieve; no, more than that. In questioning the prisoner, Alvarado had forgotten him. By tomorrow the messengers would have left and he would not be with them. Instead, he and Demonio would be going forward. He might even be riding him in battle! Already he felt the sides of the horse between his legs; the rippling of muscles, then the

long smooth gallop. No more carrying of nails for De-
monio when the trumpets blared and the drums sounded.
He could almost hear the drums now, inside his head.
Thump, thump, thump.

"Are you coming, Luis?" Bartolomé started back toward the pasture. Luis had turned to follow when a sentry
put a hand on his shoulder.

"Not you, boy. The Captain wants to speak to you."

At the door of the shelter Alvarado waited. "I had forgotten about you," he said. "I owe you some reward.
Come tell me what you wish for."

"Nothing, nothing," Luis stammered. "I only did my
duty, as did Bartolomé." The thing he most wanted was
for Alvarado to forget his existence for the next twenty-
four hours but he couldn't say that.

"Oh, nonsense. You nearly lost your life recapturing
the mare. You deserve something."

Luis twisted a finger in his tangled hair. It was damp.
Dew had begun to fall.

"You need sleep, Excellency. You just said so," he protested desperately. "Let us not talk of rewards now."

"Yes, now." Alvarado yawned again. "I find it is too
late to sleep after all. Doña Luisa has already gone to prepare chocolatl. Come inside and help me with my armor
and we will talk at the same time."

Inside the shelter a small light was burning and in one
corner was Alvarado's armor. He pointed toward it.

"The collar, boy."

While Luis fetched it, Alvarado put on a doublet with
sleeves of mail. Luis laced it for him without being asked.

"Now the cuirass." Luis fastened the straps that held breast and back plates together. His fingers needed no instruction. Alvarado nodded approvingly and returned to the question of the reward.

"Well, what do you want? Don't be shy."

Luis cast about for a reply. What would Bartolomé ask for, he wondered.

"Now the pauldrons."

Luis was lifting the pauldrons onto Alvarado's shoulders when his eyes fell on a small woven bag on the table. It was open at the top. "Beads, green beads." The words rushed to his tongue and out. "As many as Your Excellency feels right as a reward."

"Beads!" Alvarado's boisterous laugh filled the shelter. "*Por Dios*, are you an Indian to be satisfied with glass!"

Too late, Luis realized he had made a mistake. Curiosity was replacing amusement in the Captain's expression.

"Or do you intend to trade?" Alvarado asked, studying him more closely. "Who are you anyway? And to what part of my army are you attached?"

"I help Diego Sánchez, the smith," Luis replied. This much was the truth anyway.

"And from him you learned to squire an officer so well?" Alvarado shook his head. "I have seen you before but not since we set out. In Mexico. And you weren't working for any blacksmith then." Recognition began to grow in his eyes. "You were wearing silks. *Who are you? What is your name?*"

The moment could no longer be avoided. To a direct question such as this there was no evasion. And Luis could not lie. Especially to the man he admired above all others.

"My name is Luis de Lapeña." He raised his head proudly as he spoke the name for the first time in many weeks. "You saw me several times in Mexico. At the palace of the Captain-General Cortés. I was one of his pages. My father, Lorenzo de Lapeña, was his friend. Like Your Excellency and the Captain-General, he was born in the province of Estremadura."

Alvarado's brow cleared. "So that is it. Of course. I knew your father. You look like him."

Then disbelief came into his voice. "And Cortés released the son of Lorenzo de Lapeña from his service to join my army as a blacksmith's helper?"

"No, Excellency. I ran away."

"*Por Dios*, boy!" Alvarado thundered. "Didn't you think what trouble that would make for me? To give place in my army to a runaway page? And a page of the Captain-General at that!"

"I didn't think, Excellency. When the Captain-General escorted the expedition out of the city, I took off my silks and followed without his knowledge. I only intended to go a short way; to pretend to myself that I was part of the army of the great Alvarado. And, oh, Your Excellency, it was a marvelous pretense!"

Let come what might, nothing could take away the glory of those first few hours of march; before he had anything on his conscience; before he had anything to fear.

"You were riding ahead with the Captain-General," he continued. "I had intended to turn back when he did and receive whatever punishment he chose to give me. But when the time came, I knew all at once that I couldn't turn back. I had to follow you. Die for you!"

Suddenly Luis' eyes blurred. "I didn't mean to make trouble for you, Excellency. I never thought."

Was it because his eyes were blurred that he imagined a slight smirk on Alvarado's lips? Luis rubbed a dirty hand across his eyes. The smirk disappeared.

"When you send me back I will tell the Captain-General that until tonight you never knew who I was. He will believe me. I have always told him the truth."

For minutes there was silence; for Luis an agonizing silence. If Alvarado would only speak, even in anger, his misery would be more bearable.

Then the henequen curtain in front of the shelter was lifted and Doña Luisa entered, bearing a bowl of hot frothing liquid. Her high-cheeked oval face was lighter than Bartolomé's and beneath her small straight nose the lips were full and generous. She glanced inquiringly at Luis but asked no question aloud. Offering the bowl of chocolatl to Alvarado with both hands, she bowed her head in a graceful gesture. He took a loud sip. The silence was broken.

"I cannot send you back. Even Cortés would not expect me to provide you with special escort."

"But the messengers, Excellency? I could keep up with them. I am very fast." Luis swallowed to relieve the dry lump in his throat but he felt compelled to point this out.

"The runners, ah, that is unfortunate." Alvarado drained the bowl and returned it to Luisa, smiling at her. "The runners have already left—hours ago. It was to finish my report that I sat up half the night. Well, it cannot be helped. If you indeed prefer me to the Captain-General, see that you make a good soldier."

He turned away and scribbled on a piece of paper which he handed to Luis. "Run off now, and after the review give this to our notary so he may see you are properly inscribed on the rolls."

Luis felt his heart swelling. It pressed against the entire cage of his ribs. He wasn't being sent back! He was being made a regular member of the army!

"Thank you, thank you, Excellency," he cried. "And I promise never to cause you trouble again. On the contrary —" He was about to speak of the multitude of infidels he and Demonio would kill when Alvarado cut him short.

"Off with you, boy. It is nearly time to review the troops." Then, as Luis was walking away from the shelter, he called after him, "The reward for recapturing the mare must wait, but I shall not forget."

Reward? Hadn't he already been given a most wonderful reward? Luis tried to say this but Alvarado had dropped the door hanging back into place. The interview was over.

chapter

🔲🔲🔲🔲🔲🔲🔲🔲

4

No HOSTILE WARRIORS ATTACKED THE COLUMN AS IT LEFT
Soconusco next day and entered Guatemala. Luis felt
a keen sense of disappointment. He was now on the rolls as
a regular member of the expedition and he had confessed
his sins to Father Godinez. With the rest of the men, he
had taken communion that morning before setting out.
Now he was ready for action and there was none. He
longed to prove his courage in battle by some spectacular
act of daring; perhaps, even, by saving the Captain's life.

Instead he and Demonio walked behind the baggage
carriers as usual with the relay horses and their attendants.
The tall dry weeds growing on either side of the path hid
no enemy except for ticks and a possible rattler. With
Bartolomé, who marched at his side, Luis discussed his new
status.

"Once the fighting begins, Demonio will carry no more
nails. That was the agreement. Instead I will ride Demonio
in battle. I shall be a true *caballero!*" His chest lifted in
pride.

"Then I must call you *señor*." Bartolomé's black eyes looked straight ahead at the carriers. Those nearest the boys were Echeverria's Negro slaves brought from Cuba. Their backs were bent under their heavy loads of iron. Like miserable pack animals, they were driven forward by an overseer flicking a bullwhip.

"Oh no, it will not be necessary to say *señor* to me," Luis assured Bartolomé but the idea was pleasing to his vanity nonetheless. Though his eyes were on the slaves, at this moment he wasn't seeing them. Instead he saw a heap of gold and glittering jewels, high as a mountain. When he sent his share home, his mother would be pleased. And Tio Rodrigo would have to admit the stories of wealth in the New World were not exaggerated.

"As the owner of a horse I shall receive a larger share of captured treasure than a foot soldier." Luis tried to sound matter of fact but he couldn't keep an exulting tremor from his voice.

"I have heard talk," Bartolomé said hesitantly. "What if Captain Echeverria demands the return of Demonio before any treasure is divided?"

"It wouldn't matter now. It was only while I feared being sent back to Mexico that it mattered," Luis explained. "Let him ask if he wants. His Excellency wouldn't allow him to take the horse."

"Did Tonatiuh say that? When he talked to you in the shelter?"

"No, he didn't," Luis replied. "We didn't talk of Demonio. But I know he wouldn't allow it. Moreover," he added, remembering the conversation, "he asked me to name a reward for risking my life for Mamacita. I could claim his protection of my rights to Demonio as reward if necessary." This last was to convince Bartolomé only. He, Luis, knew Alvarado would uphold his rights without such a claim.

Bartolomé grunted. "Most likely Tonatiuh was thinking of a trinket."

"No, no he wasn't!" Luis started to tell about the beads and then stopped short. Alvarado had asked if he were an Indian to be satisfied with beads. He couldn't repeat that to Bartolomé.

The Indian boy looked skeptical but he dropped the subject. "A *caballero* needs armor and weapons," he said instead. "A *caballero* cannot ride in battle wearing rags."

The words deflated Luis like thorns in a puffball. He could almost feel the air rushing out of him. Picturing himself in shining metal cuirass and helmet, a long spear in one hand, urging Demonio into the thick of the fray, he had quite forgotten the clothes he was wearing. He looked down at his shirt, sweat-stained and torn by the sharp hooks of acacia bushes, and he fingered the twisted piece of cloth he wore on his head. Bartolomé was right. He needed armor, but even if it were to be had, he had no money to buy it.

For several minutes the boys trudged on in silence under the blazing sun. A slave stumbled and the bullwhip cracked.

"We must find you some armor," Bartolomé said.

"You know that is impossible." Luis' voice was bitter.

"Spanish armor, yes, but Indian armor, no. Some of the

officers, even, have adopted the quilted cotton corselets of the Indians."

It was true. In many cases heavy metal had been laid aside for the lighter but tough quilted cotton.

"We must strip an enemy warrior of his armor at the first opportunity," Bartolomé went on. "His lance and obsidian-edged broadsword too."

Luis brightened. It was after all a possibility. Cotton armor was no protection against guns but it did blunt the force of arrows.

"You will help?" he asked.

"Of course. We are friends, *sí?*" Bartolomé replied simply.

"*Sí,*" Luis agreed.

As the column wound forward, the boys were so engrossed in plans for obtaining armor that they scarcely noticed that the character of the land through which they marched had been changing. The tall weeds and dried grass and thorny bushes were giving way to larger growth. Immense ceiba trees, their feathery tops eighty feet in the air, threw more and more frequent patches of shade across the path. Then, topping a small rise of ground, Luis saw something he couldn't quite believe.

"Bartolomé, look!" He pointed. "The advance guard has disappeared."

Half a league ahead, into what seemed a solid wall of green, a company of Mexican allies was also disappearing.

Bartolomé wiped the sweat out of his eyes. "A forest," he said. "I never thought to see one again."

The march slowed to a halt and the sound of axes biting

into wood drifted back to the column's end.

"*Por Dios,* I will be glad to leave these burning plains!" Diego Sánchez, who was marching directly behind the boys voiced the opinion of the whole sun-weary army.

When marching was resumed and they, too, came to the wall, Luis saw it was actually a stand of luxurious growth bordering a dark-bottomed stream. The end of the column slowed still more to allow men and horses to drink, then splashed forward to the other bank. They had reached the beginning of the vast tropical forest through which they were to travel for the next three days.

Giant tree trunks were encircled by woody vines among which orchids flowered. Gray-green air plants hung from branches like long beards. Great ferns, verdant green and taller than a man, grew from ground that was soft underfoot. Jewel-colored moths fluttered lazily through the air and birds flying overhead were brilliant streaks of emerald, yellow, turquoise, and ruby. Small monkeys chattered like playful children as they swung on vines.

Luis drew in a lungful of moist cool air, fragrant with the scent of flowers. "It is like paradise, is it not, Bartolomé?" he breathed, stroking Demonio's sweaty neck.

"Even as to the serpent," Bartolomé grunted, pointing upward. A long thick body, tail wound around a vine, was swaying above them.

The army did not travel farther that day but made camp near the stream. That night, for the first time since leaving Mexico, Luis didn't see the stars as he lay down to sleep. Tall trees, laced together with vines, made a canopy above him, shutting out all light. The noises of the forest were unfamiliar ones: strange guttural croakings and high wild screams.

All of the horses were restless, Mamacita in particular. Luis heard her pulling against her tether rope. He began to listen more closely. There was a small rustling sound. such as a foot might make. Then came the hoot of an owl.

Luis woke Bartolomé. "Listen," he whispered. "The Quichés have sent another thief to steal Mamacita."

Bartolomé raised himself on one elbow. Both boys stopped breathing. Then Bartolomé lay down again. "The sound is not that of a man's foot but of some small animal." .

"But the owl?"

"A real owl. Perhaps Mamacita is more restless than the others because she feels the foal moving inside her. She gives birth in a few weeks. About the same time as Tia Luisa."

"Doña Luisa is to have a child!" Luis exclaimed. "I didn't know! And she has kept up with the march all these days. Why didn't she remain in Mexico?"

Bartolomé yawned. "To an Indian, birth is natural. Besides, her mule is comfortable. Tonatiuh selected it himself."

Long after Bartolomé returned to sleep, Luis remained awake, thinking of his mother. Before his little sister was born—she who had died when she was only two—his mother had rested most of every day. Even so, she had complained constantly of being tired and refused to walk farther than the church, which was no farther than Luis could throw a stone.

Early the next morning when the army set out, all the men were in good spirits. They would be protected from the sun. No matter how hot it blazed in the sky, it could not reach them except as small gold spots on the mossy ground.

By afternoon, though the jungle still seemed a world of wonder and beauty, marching through it had become a nightmare of difficulties. In a forest that grew denser the farther they penetrated, the road had been swallowed by growth. Vines caught at the chests of the horses and mangrove roots tripped them and sent them plunging to their knees. More than one horse lost a shoe in marshy ground. Ahead the allies labored to hack out a new road for the white men to follow, but even as the undergrowth yielded to their knives and axes, swarms of mosquitoes drifted back to plague the Spaniards. Snakes dispossessed of their privacy slithered underfoot.

As the soldiers dragged their feet through soggy marshes, Luis was not the only one to think nostalgically of the dry firm footing of the plains. There was no burning sun in this tropical forest, but no air either; it was like a vast sweat house. Only Alvarado seemed impervious to the hardships of travel. With a map on the pommel of his saddle and a small mariner's compass in his hand, he was everywhere, and everywhere he had words of encouragement and jokes for the men. Tired and miserable as he was, Luis' shoulders straightened every time the Captain passed. The flash of his smile was like a draught of heady wine that brought new strength to struggle forward.

Father Godinez was everywhere too, as were the other

priests. It was Father Godinez who knelt in the oozy mud to give last rites to one of Echeverria's slaves who had fallen out of the column and lay dying of snake bite.

"How goes it, son?" he asked Luis as he passed him a few minutes later.

"Pray for us, Father, and for the horses too," Luis implored. "Demonio is a mass of welts from bites, and at every step his feet are sucked down in this marsh until I fear never to see them again."

Hour after weary hour for the next two days the army pressed on through the steaming jungle, skirting swamps where they could, hacking their way through canebrakes, and fording streams. At night Luis dreamed of crocodiles staring at him with insolent eyes and would wake, covered with sweat, to hear the deep hoarse cry of a jaguar hunting in the darkness.

Still no Quiché warrior had shown himself and Luis had almost forgotten his desire to obtain armor. Indeed it seemed unlikely that he would ever need it. Like the coils of a giant anaconda, the jungle seemed to squeeze tighter and tighter around the exhausted army, threatening never to release it.

Luis' daydreams of saving Alvarado's life in battle changed to visions in which he saved him from the jaws of a crocodile or the claws of a puma.

On the afternoon of the third day the ground began to rise and they came to a swift stream with high rugged banks. For an hour before, Luis had been shaking with chills. Now his whole body was burning with fever. He scrambled down the bank and threw himself flat in the water, drinking in loud gulps until he could hold no more.

Scaling the opposite bank he held onto Demonio's tail because he felt a whirling dizziness. Suddenly his head floated upward, and looking down he saw Alvarado struggling in the grip of a fearsome animal. It had the snout of a crocodile, the coat and tail of a puma, and the legs of a horse.

"Courage! I come!" Luis cried, but now his whole body was floating in air and it would not descend.

"Luis! *Amigo!*" It was the voice of Bartolomé, calling from far below. So far below that the next time Luis heard it, the sound was only a murmur. After that he didn't hear it at all.

chapter

꧁꧁꧁꧁꧁꧁

5

"LUIS, LUIS AMIGO, OPEN YOUR MOUTH," BARTOLOME urged.

Instinctively, Luis clamped his teeth together and tightened his fever-cracked lips over them. It wasn't the first time he had heard these words in the last day and a half, and each time they had been accompanied by a bitter draught.

Luis remembered very little that had happened since he had started up the steep bank of a river, clinging to Demonio's tail. There had been periods of body-shaking chills and periods of dry burning fever and still other periods when the sweat had poured out of him. And in between, weakness and discomfort and a reluctance to focus his thoughts, like now. Luis knew they had left the jungle. He knew if he opened his eyes he would see grass instead of tangled underbrush. But he didn't want to open his eyes. If he did, Bartolomé would realize that he was awake. If he kept them closed, perhaps Bartolomé would go away without forcing him to take the medicine.

"Luis, *niño*, open your mouth." It was the other voice

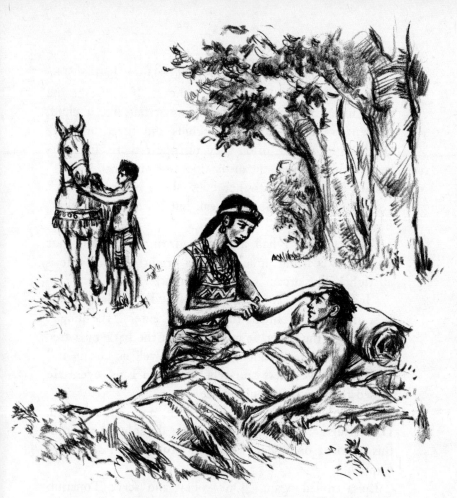

now. Soft. A woman's voice. Several times when his body was burning and his head soaring, this voice had come to him as if from a great distance.

He opened his mouth and the draught slid past his teeth and down his throat, almost choking him with its bitterness. Then he opened his eyes. Doña Luisa was kneeling beside him on the ground where he lay rolled in blankets. She put a smooth cool hand on his forehead.

"You are better, *niño*," she said. "Much better. The ague should not return for many hours. If you take the brew like a man instead of spitting it out like a child, perhaps we can hold off the chills and fever until we reach high ground; often they disappear there. It is fortunate, though, that the army does not march today."

Luis looked up into her eyes. They were like dark velvet and tender. He felt weak but his mind was clear. Fear entered into it.

"Doña Luisa, I had a terrible dream. I thought our Captain was being attacked by a frightful beast. He is all right? The dream wasn't a portent?"

"Just a dream, *niño*." She smiled. "Tonatiuh is in the best of health. From the time we first entered the jungle, I gave him the brew. It is made from the bark of a tree I know of and prevents the ague as well as curing it."

Tears of weakness and relief came to Luis' eyes. He closed them so she wouldn't see.

"I thank our Lord for his health, and I thank you, Doña Luisa, for giving us both the draught. And from this moment on I shall serve you always, as I serve our Captain."

Luisa smiled again. "Only obey and serve Tonatiuh well, and you will be serving me."

She rose and arranged her brightly woven skirt. "Now rest."

Luis watched her as she walked away and the warmth he felt in his heart was more than gratitude alone. How graceful she was. She walked with the same proud step as his mother. His mother! Suddenly, his mother's fair-skinned and rather haughty face swam before his eyes.

His mother would not be pleased to know he was comparing her to an Indian. She would be scandalized that he, a Spaniard, had sworn to serve one. Yet he felt no disloyalty to his mother in the comparison, nor did he feel that serving Doña Luisa would lessen his dignity as a Spaniard. He did not understand why this was so. He only knew it was.

Shielding Luis from the slanting sun of late afternoon was a canopy of henequen cloth stretched over poles that led to a ceiba tree. Beyond the tree he could see the camp spread out on an open plain. To the west and across a narrow stream was the rear guard. On the east bank of the stream horses were grazing or drinking. They were too far away to pick out an individual horse but several blacks moved among them. Near the horses were the baggage and the cooking fires of the allies. The forge was also there. Luis could hear the clang of hammer on anvil. Turning, he saw the four cannon set on a rise of ground, facing east. In back of them were the infantry and cavalry encampments and at a distance ahead, the advance guard. Everywhere there was a hubbub; joking and cursing mixed in rough good humor. Luis felt a rush of pride that brought with it an illusion of strength. This was his army. His!

For the past few days he hadn't been aware of its existence; now suddenly he was in a turmoil of impatience to hear everything that concerned it. He turned to Bartolomé.

"Tell me quickly what has happened since the ague struck me down. I cannot wait to know."

"Not much has happened, *amigo*," Bartolomé said with

a shrug. "Of course, many were stricken as you were. Their bodies lie rotting in the jungle, as yours would be, too, if Demonio and I hadn't carried you out."

"I thank you for that, Bartolomé," Luis said gratefully. "But is there no other news?"

"Scouts brought in three men who claimed they were gathering honey, but Tonatiuh knew them for Quiché spies."

"Did Alvarado punish them as they deserved?"

"No, he treated them kindly. He sent them to the chief of their city, Zapotitlán, with offers of friendship. He asked that the chieftains come to him and give allegiance to the king of Spain, and that they promise to give up human sacrifice and accept the True Faith."

"And did the chieftains come?" Luis' eyes were bright.

"No," Bartolomé replied. "The chieftains did not come. Nor did the spies return."

"Miserable beings," Luis cried fretfully. "Had they no gratitude for our Captain's kindness?"

Bartolomé looked away.

"What then?" Luis pressed.

"We moved forward to this camp. Beyond a deep ravine through which a river flows is Zapotitlán. From the other side of the ravine people called out to our scouts when we first arrived. They invited the army to cross over and lodge in their city, but Tonatiuh feared a trap because their chieftains hadn't come to him as he had asked."

Bartolomé stopped and put a hand between Luis' chest and the blankets. "You are swimming in sweat!" he exclaimed. He unrolled Luis' naked body and started sponging it from a bucket of lukewarm water.

"Go on, Bartolomé," Luis begged.

Bartolomé finished his task and threw a light dry cover over his patient. "Yesterday afternoon, then, Tonatiuh sent scouts to reconnoiter. Several of them were killed by arrows. Then Tonatiuh sent out some horsemen. They killed many warriors but several of our horses were wounded. This angered Tonatiuh. Today he has gone to examine the road over which we must advance. Tomorrow we march on the city."

While Bartolomé was reciting all this, excitement had been mounting in Luis. It was like a fever, except that his head was clear and his body cool. He threw off the blanket and stood up. He felt a slight dizziness but in a moment it passed, as the trembling in his legs passed too.

"If we march on the city tomorrow, I need armor to ride in! Have you forgotten, Bartolomé? Let us search quickly among yesterday's dead."

"You would go naked to search for armor?" Bartolomé asked.

"Of course not." Luis looked around him on the ground. "Where are my clothes?"

"Tia Luisa gave them to her servant to wash. They will be returned this evening."

"But I must have armor and weapons!" Luis' voice was high with exasperation. "I shall wear a loincloth." He reached for the woven henequen that had shaded him.

"And on your feet?"

"You promised to help, Bartolomé. Lend me your sandals. Often you go without, by choice."

"No, Luis, I will not lend them."

"*Por favor, amigo!*"

"No."

Luis' lips stiffened in anger. "And what if I command you?"

The boys glared at each other with hostile eyes, all friendship forgotten in one moment. It seemed to Luis an hour that they stood so, watching each other like gamecocks, before he began to feel shame.

"I am sorry, Bartolomé," he said at last. "The sandals are yours and I had no right to command."

Bartolomé looked at the ground then. "It was not a question of sandals, Luis," he explained with dignity, "but of your health. Besides, you have no need for armor. You will not ride tomorrow."

"But Doña Luisa said the ague might not return at all if I take the draughts. I will drink double tonight. And see how firm my legs are. I feel entirely well."

"Even so, you will not ride."

"But why, Bartolomé? Luis turned so that he could see the grazing horses. His eyebrows drew together in a worried frown. "Is Demonio lame? Has he lost another shoe?"

Bartolomé looked away across the plain. "He is not lame. He has four shoes."

"Then why?" Luis persisted.

Bartolomé sighed—a deep sigh that came from the bottom of his stomach. "You will not ride, Luis, because you have no horse. Last night Captain Echeverria took him back."

chapter

🪟🪟🪟🪟🪟🪟🪟🪟

6

AT FIRST BARTOLOMÉ'S WORDS HAD STUNNED LUIS, AS A blow on the head might have done. Then, regaining sense and speech, he had rejected them.

"It isn't true, Bartolomé, it isn't true!"

"It is true, *amigo*. Captain Echeverria's horse was one of those wounded yesterday afternoon."

Then had come words of recrimination, bitter as the drug made from bark. "You call me *amigo* and you let Demonio be taken from me while I lay sick!"

"I was not with the horses last night. I was here with you. But had I been roped to Demonio, I could have done nothing. Señor Echeverria is an officer."

"You could have appealed to our Captain," Luis accused.

Bartolomé looked surly. "Tonatiuh's mind is on the taking of Zapotitlán," he said.

"I will go to him myself when he returns to camp. By then I shall have clothes to wear and need not beg for yours. He will order Echeverria to give back Demonio.

You will see."

Bartolomé made no reply.

That evening, dressed in his newly washed clothes, boots shining and soft with grease, Luis went to the rise of ground beside the cannon where a soldier told him he would find Alvarado. A guard stopped him.

"I must see His Excellency." Luis' voice was urgent. "It is a matter of great importance."

"His Excellency is occupied. Can't you see that, boy?" The guard made no move to let him pass.

But he *must* get past! He had to tell Alvarado how Demonio had been taken from him by Echeverria. Luis thought quickly. Perhaps mention of the reward would impress the guard.

"His Excellency promised me a reward. He asked me to name it. I have come to do so." Luis said all this as loud as he could, hoping his words would carry even beyond the guard, to the Captain himself. Luis could see him standing at the very top of the small mound where the cannon were mounted, talking to some officers. But Alvarado didn't look in his direction; he couldn't have heard. And the guard was not impressed.

He turned Luis around and gave him a shove. "Be off and do not return. Until Zapotitlán is captured, His Excellency sees no one but his officers. It is an order."

Luis knew there was no use protesting. He walked slowly back toward the shelter, hoping Bartolomé wouldn't be there. Having boasted, he didn't wish to talk about his failure. On the way he passed the cavalry encampment. Behind it the horses that were to be used the next morning were picketed. Although it was fast growing dark, he had no difficulty in recognizing Demonio. The horse recognized him too, giving a soft nicker of welcome.

Luis went up to him and laid his face against the soft muzzle. "It is not my fault, *amigo mio*," he whispered. "Do not blame me when Echeverria mounts you tomorrow. You will not have to put up with him long. After the city is captured, you will be mine again. No one can keep me from our Captain then."

A hand grasped Luis' collar and lifted him high off the ground. "Stand back from Captain Echeverria's horse!" It was the man who drove Echeverria's slaves on the march. The order was followed by an obscene oath, and then the hand released its hold and Luis fell.

Picking himself up, he went on, walking unsteadily now. He felt weak and a little light-headed as though the fever were returning. At the shelter he was glad to find Bartolomé, after all. Bartolomé didn't ask any questions. He held out a gourd and Luis gulped its bitter contents gratefully.

After Mass the next morning the army broke camp and moved out toward the ravine that lay, less than a league away, between Alvarado's forces and the city of Zapotitlán.

First the advance guard moved out, then the main body of cavalry, and then the infantry with Alvarado riding at its head. Echeverria, on Demonio, led one company of infantry. He sat the horse stiffly but seemed to be having no trouble. Luis was glad of this for Demonio's sake but it was hard to see such a one on his back.

Behind the Spanish foot soldiers the allies fell in, and then came the baggage carriers and the men leading the relay horses. Today, Doña Luisa rode among these, protected by the rear guard. It was her usual position except in times of no danger. Bartolomé walked on one side of her mule and Luis on the other while her woman servant followed.

"How are you feeling, *niño?*" Doña Luisa asked, looking down at Luis.

"*Muy bién, gracias,*" he replied. "I feel well, Doña Luisa, but not happy. Did you know Echeverria took Demonio from me while I was sick?"

"I didn't know." Her voice was distressed.

"I tried to tell our Captain, but a guard kept me from him."

"Perhaps tonight you can reach his ear," she suggested.

It was a kind thought but not very comforting. By tonight the battle he longed to ride in would be over.

Soon after they left camp they came onto a broad highway leading toward the city. It was easy on the feet and the morning was still cool.

"Better than the swamp, eh?" The blacksmith's voice sounded cheerful.

"I shall not care if I never see another crocodile." Bartolomé was also cheerful, but Luis could not make himself feel anything but glum.

A little farther on, the road ran between trees that Luis had never seen before. Pods of reddish color grew close together on branches that were lower than a horse's head.

"Cacao," Doña Luisa said, peering anxiously into the grove. "It was from there the Quiché warriors shot at our horsemen yesterday. They could not pursue the Quichés because of the trees. God grant no enemy hides there now."

This danger was also anticipated by Jorge Alvarado, one of the Captain's brothers, who commanded the rear guard and now brought it close around the baggage. From ahead came the sharp crack of muskets and the roar of cannon. Automatically steps, even those of the heavy-laden baggage carriers, began to quicken, but when they came out of the cacao into the open Jorge ordered a halt. The ravine was about four bowshots away and by looking between the heads of those in front, Luis caught a glimpse of the main army advancing toward it.

Then the command came to form a square. Gold, powder, and horseshoes were placed on the ground in the middle of it. The relay horses, with their attendants, and Doña Luisa and her woman were also put on the inside. Next were the slaves and Indian baggage carriers, and on the outside, the fighting men.

An officer came up to Luis and Bartolomé. "Follow me," he ordered and led them out of the square. He took them to the front of it where Luis saw some of the other younger attendants had already been placed among the soldiers. All were standing two arm-lengths apart. The officer gave Luis and Bartolomé each a spear.

"This will be your post," he said. "It needs less protection than the rear but it is still important. We wait here until the ravine is taken. In the meantime there is always danger of attack on the baggage."

Luis handled his spear. Its broad edge was set with chips of sharp obsidian. A Quiché weapon, and a deadly one. It was the sort he'd hoped yesterday to find for himself; the kind he'd hoped to carry while riding Demonio in battle. The feel of it increased his bitterness against Echeverria and his longing to be in the fighting. Guarding the baggage at a safe distance was a dull substitute.

From this new position Luis could see the battle in progress.

A narrow wooden bridge spanned the ravine and a large body of Quiché warriors were defending it fiercely. Their arrows were launched against the Spaniards in a ceaseless rain. Cries of defiance mingled with screams of rage and pain as the Quichés were mowed down by musket fire, but even as their bodies hurtled down into the gorge below, other warriors took their places on the bridge.

On the far side of the ravine rose a cliff, and all along the top of this Luis saw that breastworks made of touching shields commanded river and bridge. Even when the bridge was captured, crossing would not be safe until these breastworks were also taken, and the cannon directed toward them seemed to be doing little damage.

The cavalry waited. All of the horses were cavorting impatiently. The musket fire grew sharper. The Quichés on the bridge were thinning. Suddenly the firing stopped and some of the allies rushed out on the bridge, clearing it of bodies.

A bugle sounded and the cavalry advanced toward the bridge in columns of twos. Just as the first platoon crossed over, a riderless horse came galloping back toward the baggage. A black horse.

Was it? Yes! It was Demonio! As he came rushing forward, Luis stepped in front of him. The horse stopped short, reared, and blew out sharply through his nostrils.

"Quiet, Demonio." Luis spoke soothingly, though his heart was pounding with excitement. "Stand still, *amigo mio*. It is I who will ride you now."

Demonio was covered with sweat and a trickle of blood ran from the edge of his mouth where the bit had cut into it. His eyes rolled, whites showing. He continued to snort and toss his head, but after a little he allowed Luis to mount him.

There had been no time for conscious decision. One moment Luis had been longing to be part of the battle and the next he was rushing toward it. The bridge, so narrow that there was room for only two horses abreast, was suddenly right ahead of him. He was swept into the rear of a column and onto the bridge. Half way over Demonio slipped in a puddle of blood and veered toward the edge. For one awful moment Luis looked down at the water swirling far below him; then Demonio recovered himself and plunged forward. Something bit at Luis' shoulder but he hardly noticed. On the other side of

the bridge they clambered up a steep bank in any order they could, the horses slipping and sliding as stones rolled under their feet. For a brief minute Luis found himself riding next to Don Pedro Puertocarrero. The man threw him a startled glance.

"*Por Dios*, boy, what are you doing here? And are you mad that you ride without armor?"

For the first time Luis gave thought to his vulnerable condition and the blood streaming down his arm, but there was nothing he could do about either.

"I trust in God," he replied with a confidence he was far from feeling.

"May He protect you!" Don Pedro shouted as he surged ahead.

Cannon roared and arrows whistled but they seemed of less importance than keeping Demonio on his feet. Then at last they were at the top of the cliff on a broad plateau. Ahead, Luis saw Indians put to flight by the first platoon, running helter-skelter toward the city. The cavalry pursued for a short distance and then drew rein. The first company, under Captain Chávez, rode off to the right. Luis had no idea what he was supposed to do but he followed Puertocarrero to the left. They took up a gallop at single file.

"Ta-taa! Ta-taa!" The bugle ended on a low note.

They wheeled, each horse to the left, making a straight line.

"Ta-taa! Ta-taa! Ta-taa!"

"*Santiago y a ellos!*" The cry rose from every throat as the horsemen charged, spears pointing forward, sun glinting on spear tips.

There was no time for fear. Luis felt only the reckless intoxication of excitement and speed. The beat of his heart and the beat of hoofs were one. He scarcely had time to see the warriors at the plateau's edge when the cavalry was on them.

The warriors who had commanded the ravine from behind their breastworks of shields were now trapped between cliff and cavalry. Faced with a choice, many chose the cliff rather than the frightful four-footed gods.

They threw themselves over, leaping far out into space, disappearing while their shrieks still made the air hideous with sound.

Some though, with courage born of desperation, stood their ground. It was close combat in terrible confusion. Even now, Luis wasn't conscious of danger as much as the smell—a sickening odor of sweat and grease. He didn't notice the warrior at his stirrup until a voice warned him.

"Watch out, boy."

Instinctively he wheeled Demonio and brought him up in a rear. Descending, his spear cut through quilted armor and the Indian fell. It was the force of Demonio's descent rather than Luis' strength that had given power to the blow.

As he drew the spear out, there came a gurgle from the Indian's throat and a rush of blood. Luis swayed in the saddle and tasted vomit in his mouth. He had never killed a man before.

chapter

🔲🔲🔲🔲🔲🔲🔲🔲

7

NOT A WARRIOR REMAINED ALIVE WHEN THE CAVALRY finished its work. The Quiché bows that had launched such a devastating rain of arrows on the bridge and ravine lay broken beneath the hoofs of the Spaniards' horses. Most of the round shields were broken too, and trampled into the blood-soaked grass were headdresses resembling the snouts of animals and the tails of birds, with strands of hair and bits of flesh still clinging to them.

From the saddle Luis looked down at the ground with an almost overpowering feeling of revulsion. The blue-eyed, dark-bearded young giant standing at Demonio's stirrup had to speak twice before Luis paid attention.

"Bravely fought, young one." It was the same voice that had given him warning a few minutes earlier.

To Luis' battle-deafened ears, the words of praise seemed to come from miles away. Later he would treasure them but now he wasn't quite sure the words weren't part of returning fever. Still, a man must reply politely even in a dream.

"I thank the *señor* . . ." He swayed in the saddle.

"Alonso Rojas." The man supplied his name. Then, eyes on Luis' shirt sleeve, he said in a different voice, "You are hurt, by the looks of it. Get down and let me examine your wound."

Luis slid off Demonio's back. "It is nothing, an arrow at the bridge. I scarcely noticed it."

Rojas stripped off Luis' shirt and bathed the wound with some fiery liquid from his flask. In spite of himself, Luis cried out at the pain. Rojas grunted reassuringly, "You are right. The wound is not serious but the next time you may not be so lucky."

He tore a piece of material from the shirt and bound it over the wound. "There is nothing more for us to do until the main army comes up with us. We are well beyond arrow shot from any cover and it isn't likely the enemy will try to attack us in the open. You had better use this opportunity to find yourself some armor. God knows there is plenty lying about."

Luis glanced at the sprawling dead bodies, their faces grimacing up at the sun. He did not want to touch one but the eyes of Rojas were on him and he was ashamed to admit squeamishness. He chose a long quilted cotton tunic that looked less foul than the others nearby and pulled it off over the Indian's head. He was sure he was going to be sick as he struggled into it himself.

"Here is a shield that will do." The man handed him one spattered with gore. Suddenly blue eyes and dark curling beard whirled crazily around and Luis saw, instead, the clay-painted face of the savage who had tried to kill him. He could control his stomach no longer.

"No need to be ashamed," Rojas laughed. "This is your first battle, no doubt. I am not so old that I have forgotten my own. I'm curious, though. How comes it that . . ."

"Rojas!" a voice bellowed from farther down the line.

"I come," Rojas shouted in answer. Then to Luis, "Good fortune ride with you, young one." Leading his horse, a ewe-necked roan, he left.

Luis cleaned himself as best he could with grass. Then, loosening Demonio's girth and looping his reins over one arm, he went to stand near some other horsemen at the cliff's edge. The battle was still going on in the ravine. He watched, once more from a distance, as when he'd stood guarding the baggage and the relay horses. Only now he felt no frantic urge to be in the thick of it. He was shaking all over and not sure whether it was from exhaustion or fear. He wondered if when the time came to mount again, he would have the courage he needed.

Below him a company of infantry and a large number of allies were attempting to clear the woods of Quiché warriors who were fighting from behind trees and boulders. There was some musket fire but for the most part it was a battle by sword and arrow. The trees were too close-growing for horses to be of use, so the officers, too, were on foot. Luis thought at one moment that he saw Echeverria, then a treetop hid the man and he couldn't be sure.

While leaning forward to get a better view he heard
some men come up behind him and dismount. They
were talking and Luis recognized two of the voices,
though he didn't look around.

"Holy Mother, what a slaughter we have just in-
flicted. It is hard not to be sorry for the poor savages."
That was Captain Cardona, a man with a lumpish figure
who rode with no elegance but had the reputation for
great courage.

"You're as soft on Indians as our Fray Pontaza and
that crazy Las Casas, whose words he always tries to
ram down our gullets," Conzalo Alvarado replied jeer-
ingly.

Luis didn't like Gonzalo as he liked Jorge and the
Captain's other brothers, but he agreed that to be sorry
for such murderous savages was soft. Fray Pontaza, of
whom Gonzalo had just spoken, was one of the two
Franciscans who accompanied the expedition. The other
name, Las Casas, Luis didn't recognize.

"In any event, since brother Pedro has ordered slaves
made of all the savages taken alive, they are better off
dead than captured." Gonzalo paused, then added grimly,
"As we will be, too, if it comes to that."

Across the ravine the baggage carriers and relay horses
were moving slowly toward the bridge, shepherded by
the rear guard.

"I am of your opinion on that, Gonzalo," a third voice
spoke up. "I was in Mexico at the time of the 'Noche
Triste' when Spanish captives were sacrificed to Huit-
zilopotchli. Their hearts were torn out while still beat-

ing. They say the Quiché god, Tohil, demands human sacrifice also."

Luis felt the sweat on the back of his neck turn cold. Before Mexico was finally conquered the Spanish army had been forced, at one time, to withdraw from Montezuma's city. Luis had heard, of course, of the terrible sacrificing that followed this retreat on the Night of Sorrow but it had never occurred to him that he might face the same fate in Guatemala. There was no doubt about fear now. It crawled over his body like an army of lice. Why hadn't he thought to find out more about the Quichés before he'd left Mexico?

Far below, Pedro Alvarado galloped along the edge of the ravine, directing the fighting. He looked as small as a toy soldier but there was no mistaking his identity. An arrow struck his helmet and before it could fall to the ground, he grasped it by the shank and waved it in what appeared a gay salute.

Luis felt a hot surge of courage rise up in him. Even if he had known of the Quichés' bloodthirsty god, Tohil, he would still have followed Alvarado. Nothing could have stopped him.

So much had gone through Luis' mind in so short a time that Cardona's next words seemed minutes rather than seconds later.

"The more reason, then, to teach the Quichés the True Faith and the humane laws of Spain. At present they know no better than to worship Tohil."

"This hypocrisy makes me sick," Gonzalo sneered. "Conversion and teaching them better ways of life!

Bah! It is gold the King wants, gold we all want. Nothing else matters."

"It is well for you that your brother Pedro did not hear that remark." Cardona's voice rose in anger.

"My dear brother Pedro is the worst hypocrite of all," Gonzalo declared. "He talks of conversion but thinks of nothing but gain. His gain."

Luis couldn't listen in silence any longer. He turned and faced the men standing behind him, leaning against their horses.

"It isn't so! How can you say such a thing?" he demanded.

An amused smile lit the cruel dark face of Gonzalo Alvarado. "Holy Mother, what have we here? A child, no less, who rushes to the defense of my brother." Then his eyes narrowed as they went past Luis to Demonio. As he seemed about to speak again, a great shout of victory arose from the ravine and was taken up by the cavalry on the plateau.

Gonzalo, Cardona, and their companion mounted and galloped off.

The firing had ceased. With screams and yells the enemy scattered and were fleeing in disorder up the river.

Luis' heart was still seething against Gonzalo as he watched allies and infantrymen scramble up the steep side of the ravine.

The main army began to cross the bridge. A platoon of infantry, then the cannon, then more infantry. A few arrows whizzed above their heads but did no harm. Then came the baggage carriers and the relay horses.

Luis saw the long ears of Doña Luisa's mule bobbing among them. Alvarado himself remained behind with the rear guard until all others were safely over.

At last the whole army was reassembled on the plateau above the ravine. At a distance Luis saw Bartolomé standing near Doña Luisa. He longed to speak to him; to share with him his anger against Gonzalo; to tell how he, Luis, had killed an infidel. But there was no time. Alvarado had already begun to draw up his ranks. As the cavalry moved out, Luis found himself riding knee to knee with Alonso Rojas.

"How goes it, young one?"

"*Muy bién, señor.*" But he didn't feel that all was well. Courage was slipping away once more.

"And your stomach?" Rojas teased.

"It will not act so childishly again." It was churning about even as Luis spoke.

With the cliff at its back, the army swept across open ground. Ahead lay the city of Zapotitlán, a quarter of a league off, but growing closer every minute. Luis wished it were farther away. He was not ready yet.

Then they were on it and the enemy ran out from their houses, screaming and shooting arrows.

A warrior seized Rojas by the leg while he was directing a thrust at a savage on his other side. He was almost torn from the saddle when Luis noticed what was going on.

"Up, Demonio!" he shouted, tapping his shoulder, and when the horse came down the warrior was crushed under his hoofs.

"*Gracias, amigo*," Rojas called over his shoulder as he spurred forward.

Luis didn't know whether he killed more Indians or not that afternoon. He only knew that all fear had left him and whenever a savage stood in his way he rode him down.

In the meantime the infantry and the artillery had come up. As the guns spoke, the Quichés quit the city and rushed for the woods beyond. For half a league Alvarado gave the allies leave to pursue and kill.

When the city had been cleared of the dead, the army made camp in the abandoned market place, bringing grass in from the plains for the horses to eat. And not for a long time had the men eaten so well themselves, because the people of Zapotitlán had left an abundance of food behind them.

After he had seen to Demonio's comfort, Luis looked for Alonso Rojas. He found him sitting with some other cavalrymen around a cooking fire, dipping flat cakes of cornmeal into a pot of rich-smelling meat and gravy. Luis' mouth began to water as he came to stand behind him.

Rojas looked up with a smile. "This is the brave lad I told you about," he said to a companion, then turned to Luis. "Is there anything I can do for you, young one?"

"Yes!" Luis' heart cried out silently. "You can ask me to stay and share food with you." But, of course, he couldn't say this out loud.

"*Gracias, señor*, there is nothing," he said instead. "I only wished to make sure all was well with you. Now I return to eat with my friends."

Head held high, he crossed the square to another fire and squatted down beside Bartolomé. The Tlascalan greeted him stiffly.

"Now that you ride with the cavalry, I am surprised that you seek my company."

Luis took a leg of wild turkey that the man at the spit offered him and bit into it. "You are my friend," he said, wiping his mouth. "I do not forget this just because I ride."

He hoped that Bartolomé didn't guess just how ready he'd been to forget it only minutes before. Reaching forward, he selected a ripe plum from a woven platter.

"I see you are wearing armor." Bartolomé's voice was less constrained now. "Is it from a warrior you killed?"

"No, but I killed many today." The desire to boast quickened in Luis, lessening his disappointment at not being asked to share the cavalry mess. While Bartolomé listened with his whole attention, Luis magnified his deeds until it seemed the conquest of Zapotitlán must have surely failed except for him.

"And were you not afraid?" Bartolomé asked when he had brought the account to an end.

"Afraid?" Luis repeated scornfully. "Afraid of what? Have I not the best horse in the entire army? And tonight I will go to our Captain and claim him."

It was at this moment that Diego Sánchez laid a hand on his shoulder. "I have been searching for you, *chico*," he said. "Pedro Alvarado has sent for you. His quarters are by the temple."

Luis jumped up, cheeks flushed with pride and eyes shining with eagerness.

"Oh, Bartolomé," he cried when the blacksmith had left, "our Captain must have heard how I distinguished myself today. Perhaps it means a promotion. After tonight Echeverria will never dare to lay hand on Demonio again. It is I who will ride him always. I, Luis de Lapeña!"

chapter

8

ALVARADO HAD CHOSEN FOR HIS HEADQUARTERS ONE OF the larger houses, that of a noble, a long one-story building with a thatched roof. Beside it a pyramid-shaped structure rose fifty feet in the air, stone steps leading up it to the temple on its flat top. Even though Luis' spirits were high in anticipation of the promotion that was more than a "perhaps" in his mind, goose pimples rose on his skin as he passed beneath the temple. It was there, had the battle gone otherwise, that the Spaniards might have been sacrificed.

In front of Alvarado's quarters Luis was stopped by a guard who obviously expected him.

"Wait here, boy. His Excellency has not yet finished eating."

Voices and hearty coarse laughter came from inside the building. By the sound, there were many officers with Alvarado and all in high good humor but their jokes didn't interest Luis, so he didn't listen closely. He was putting words together in his mind; words of response to the praise that would be given him for his valor in battle.

"It was nothing, Excellency," he would say modestly. "It was the horse, Demonio, who deserves the credit. I only ask that you confirm my right to him so we may always ride together in the cavalry to serve you and the King."

When Luis had settled on this speech he became impatient of the delay and started fidgeting with his clothes. His shirt was sweaty and rumpled and the shoulder was stained brown with dried blood. He wished he'd taken the time he'd already spent waiting to borrow a clean shirt. Diego Sánchez had three and would have surely loaned him one for so important an occasion.

At length men began coming from the building, belching and picking their teeth as they set off across the fast-darkening market place. These were Alvarado's top officers: such men as Chávez, Cardona, and Dardón. One stopped and spoke to the guard, who a moment later came over to Luis.

"His Excellency is ready for you now."

Luis' heart quickened as he entered the building.

Alvarado was seated at a table covered with a handsome embroidered cloth, at each end of which torches flamed. Indian servants, naked except for breechclouts, were clearing away plates that shone like silver.

Luis bowed low, received a nod of recognition, and then stood at attention while Alvarado reached for a reddish brown plum and ate it slowly.

Though most of the officers had left, three still re-

mained: Puertocarrero, Gonzalo Alvarado, and Echeverria. Gonzalo and Echeverria were looking at him in an unfriendly way and Luis did not wish to return the look, so he gazed fixedly over their heads at the frescoed wall behind them. He felt embarrassed by their presence. He had not expected others at this interview.

Perphaps, though, Alvarado was waiting for them to leave. This might be why he was taking so long to eat one plum. Under his breath Luis started rehearsing his speech again. "It was nothing, Excellency. It was the horse, Demonio, who deserves—"

"Luis de Lapeña," Alvarado's voice cut into the speech, "you are here to answer charges brought against you. The first is of disobeying orders by deserting your post during the battle this morning. The second is of converting to your own use without authority the horse of an officer. How do you plead? Innocent or guilty?"

The words were so unexpected and incredible that Luis could only suck in breath in a great gulp.

"How do you plead?" Alvarado asked again, impatiently.

Plead! Innocent or guilty! It must be that the fever had come back—that he was imagining all this, Luis thought wildly.

Then Puertocarrero spoke. "Give the lad time, Pedro. As you can see, these charges are a shock. He is young and impetuous. He only sought action when he left his post."

Puertocarrero's voice was too reasonable to be fantasy, and also what he said. So it couldn't be the fever. Someone had actually brought these terrible charges against him. Who? His eyes went to Echeverria.

Luis' wits returned. The charges wouldn't be sustained. What Puertocarrero said was true. It *had* been to seek action that he'd left the place assigned to him where there had been no hope of any. Demonio had come galloping up, he'd mounted, and he'd served the army well in battle. Surely the Captain would see it this way too.

"And as for the second charge," Puertocarrero went on, "as to that—"

"Don't try to find excuses there, Puertocarrero," Echeverria interrupted. "I had dismounted to tighten my girth and the horse broke loose. He'd gone only a short way when this undisciplined young cockerel seized him and rode off. *Converting to his own use!*" Echeverria spat on the floor. "A plague on such fancy words. It was theft no less. Moreover, in riding the horse the boy interfered with the action of the cavalry. Gonzalo told me this."

"And I deny it," Puertocarrero growled.

Luis' eyes had not left Echeverria's face since the man first started speaking. His expression was arrogant. And why not, with the Captain's own brother backing him? Gonzalo must have recognized Demonio as they stood at the cliff's edge, and later he and Echeverria had concocted this story of interference to prejudice Alvarado.

Luis opened his lips to cry out with all the violent anger he felt at this injustice. He hadn't been in the way! He had saved the life of Rojas and killed more than his share of infidels! Then reason stopped him. Demonio was at stake. A show of rage wouldn't help his case. Undoubtedly it was what Echeverria hoped for.

"Gentlemen, enough of this." Alvarado had reached the end of his patience. "The boy has had time now to gather his wits. How do you plead, Lapeña? Innocent or guilty?"

Luis gave Echeverria a last long look in which scorn and hatred were mingled, then turned his eyes to Alvarado.

"I am ready to answer the charges, Excellency," he said with what calmness he could muster. "Of the first

I am guilty; of the second, innocent. I had no need for authority to take the horse. He belongs to me. It was Captain Echeverria who took him without leave while I lay sick with fever."

Alvarado leaned forward, placing both elbows on the table. "Not so fast, Lapeña. Do you fully understand the first charge, to which you have just pled guilty? I want no accusation of unfairness later."

"I did leave my post, Excellency. If I said otherwise I would be lying. But about the horse—Captain Echeverria gave him to me at Tonalá. He could not control him and was nearly killed. When the horse ran off to the plains, he offered him to anyone who brought saddle and bridle back. I did so and reminded him of his offer. He said, 'Take him and be damned!' "

"I heard Echeverria say it." Puertocarrero confirmed the statement.

Luis gave him a look of gratitude and rushed on. "If your Excellency remembers, you promised me a reward for catching the Quiché spy who stole the mare Mamacita. I have not claimed it yet. I ask now that—"

Alvarado cut him off. "This is a court, Lapeña. We are here to establish truth, not to distribute rewards." He turned to Echeverria. "What do you say to Puertocarrero's testimony?"

"A barefaced lie, Pedro. The horse acted badly at Tonalá and I turned him over to the boy to be trained, as I had no time for it myself. There was no question of gift. Gonzalo will bear me out on this."

"I will indeed. Echeverria promised the boy fifty

maravedis if he trained him well."

"It isn't so!" Luis burst out, forgetting his determination to remain calm.

Alvarado ignored the outburst and addressed himself to his officers. "This is a matter that requires thought, gentlemen." His fingers played with the long gold chain he wore around his neck. "The charge depends on ownership of the horse. Now my brother Gonzalo, who is of undisputed honor, supports Echeverria in his claim to the animal."

"I knew you would see it that way, Pedro." Echeverria's lips drew back from long yellow teeth in a smile of satisfaction. "And henceforth I will teach the brute obedience myself if I have to flay all the hide off his body."

"No!" Luis cried. "No, no, no!"

"Silence!" Alvarado thundered. Then he continued in an even voice as though there had been no interruption. "On the other hand, Don Pedro de Puertocarrero, who is also of undisputed honor, supports the boy."

"The lad speaks the truth," Puertocarrero asserted.

"Therefore, if I took either side it would appear I doubted the word of one or the other of these honorable officers. For this reason there will be no decision on the second charge. To settle the question for all time, I am buying the horse for myself."

"I am not satisfied." Echeverria's voice was sour.

"You will be," Alvarado assured him blandly. "You already own two and one-tenth shares in the expedition. After the King's fifth has been paid, that gives you more than a fiftieth part of all treasure taken. For your claim on the animal, I will raise your number of shares to two and one-quarter. Agreed?"

"Agreed," Echeverria said, his eyes narrowing with avarice. "The brute is worthless anyway. So long as he is not given to the boy, I don't care what becomes of him."

"And you, Lapeña. For your claim you shall have four ducats."

"I don't want the money," Luis said unhappily. "It would be like selling a friend."

Alvarado nodded to the men at the table. "The matter is concluded, gentlemen. You may leave."

As the officers rose, Luis turned to follow them out of the building. His eyes were on the ground, his heart as heavy as the load Echeverria's slaves carried. The verdict had been just. Between the two stories he couldn't have judged himself if he hadn't known the truth. But to give up Demonio even to the man he most admired wasn't easy.

At the threshold Alvarado stopped him. "Not you, Lapeña. To the first charge you pled guilty. For that you must be flogged."

Flogged! Luis winced as though the lash had already bitten into his flesh, tearing it apart as it had the flesh of the Quiché thief. A flogging! He'd completely forgotten the first charge and surely it didn't merit such punishment.

Puertocarrero came back into the room. "Be easy on him, Pedro. He rode bravely today. He's a good lad."

"Softness will make him no better," Alvarado said sternly. "He was assigned a post to protect the baggage. It was attacked soon after the cavalry crossed the bridge. It makes no difference that he rode bravely. His absence left a hole in the defense."

Luis drew his breath in sharply. Why hadn't Bartolomé told him this? Because his own boasting had left no opportunity? He felt a sense of shame stronger than his fear of the lash, though the Holy Mother knew how much he dreaded it. Doña Luisa had been with the baggage. He had sworn to serve her always and the first time there had been need of his protection, he'd failed.

"But, Pedro, he is only a boy," Puertocarrero protested.

"He is a member of my army," Alvarado replied, "and discipline is necessary. Without it we could never have come this far in safety nor would we ever conquer Guatemala. What do you say, Lapeña? Are you a child to be coddled, or a man?"

Luis straightened his shoulders. "I am a man, Excellency, and the punishment is deserved."

When Puertocarrero had left, Alvarado spoke again and his voice had lost its sternness. "In time, Luis, you will make a soldier of whom your father would have been proud. In time, when you have learned discipline, I may let you ride with the cavalry. I am sorry about that horse of yours but you may still have the care of him."

That horse of yours, Alvarado had said. *That horse of yours*. Luis stared. It couldn't be true.

"You knew he was mine?" No, it couldn't be true.

The Captain would say it wasn't.

Alvarado didn't answer. But in his face Luis read that this incredible thing was so.

"You knew all along." At first, the realization numbed Luis; he felt sick and confused. Then blood rushed wildly to his head.

"You knew! Why did you pretend you didn't?" His voice rose and cracked. "The decision was unfair—it wasn't fair!"

"I did what had to be done. It is not for you to question," Alvarado said coldly. Then abruptly he smiled. "Now about the reward for saving the mare. I haven't forgotten. What do you ask?"

"I ask for justice!" Luis' eyes blazed.

"The horse, Demonio? Impossible. But a remitment of punishment? That I could grant."

"If I can't have justice, I ask for nothing."

"As you wish, my hotheaded young friend," Alvarado replied.

For a long moment the man and boy stared at each other. On Luis' face was a look of defiance; on Alvarado's, one of exasperation. The man turned away first. He gave a short laugh.

"Well, since it's your choice, take off your shirt. I'll send in a guard to lay on your punishment."

The flogging was with a belt, not the cruel lash that Luis had expected. It raised welts on his back but was no more severe than beatings Tio Rodrigo had given him more than once since the death of his father. As the strap came down again and again, the pain was great but not great enough to blot out thinking. Instead, the strokes seemed to underscore the one thought he would have given anything to forget. He had been betrayed. And by Pedro de Alvarado.

Luis didn't cry out once during the flogging, but later, outside in the dark, tears ran down his cheeks. He had lost more than Demonio. There was a terrible emptiness in his heart.

He skirted the embers of the cooking fires where soldiers still talked or played at dice and made for the far end of the market place where the horses were picketed. Bartolomé fell into step beside him.

"I have heard, *amigo*," he said.

Luis didn't answer and Bartolomé only spoke again to indicate where he had spread their blankets by Mamacita and Demonio.

chapter

꿰꿰꿰꿰꿰꿰꿰

9

EVERY TIME DURING THE NIGHT THAT LUIS TURNED ON his back, pain would waken him. At first he always felt a flood of relief. It had been a nightmare. Then slowly and relentlessly full consciousness would return. No, it hadn't been a dream. It had really happened and never again would anything be the same. Luis knew this. He also knew that he would never tell anyone how Alvarado had betrayed him. Not even to Father Godinez would he ever talk about it.

At last he opened his eyes to the gray light of early morning instead of darkness. From across the square came the drone of voices. Luis caught a word or two. Prayers used in Mass for the dead. Two soldiers had received mortal wounds during the battle. The second— the one who had lingered—must have died during the night.

Near at hand, the horses, hungry for grass, were paw- ing the ground impatiently. Luis rose stiffly and went to Demonio, laying his face against the horse's soft muzzle. As always, he felt a current of love flow between them, but now it brought only added pain.

"Do you know you are no longer mine, *amigo?* That though I may care for you, I will never ride you again?"

Demonio gave a soft whinny but it was one of pleasure. No, he hadn't understood.

Bartolomé was already up and picking thorns out of the tail of Mamacita, talking to her soothingly in the language of Tlascala. When he noticed Luis, he broke off.

"My heart is heavy for you," he said.

"*Gracias.*" Luis' voice scratched in his throat.

"As soon as scouts return and say it is safe, the horses will be allowed out to graze. I have brushed Demonio for you."

"*Gracias.*"

Bartolomé pulled a few more thorns loose. Then, eyes still on the tail, he said, "From now on, Demonio will not be obliged to carry Captain Echeverria. That, at least, is good."

"Yes."

"Tonatiuh rides well. He does not abuse his horses. That too is good."

"I know."

Bartolomé was only seeking reasons to console him for the loss of Demonio, Luis knew, but it was becoming harder and harder to answer.

Luis hoped that word would come to lead the horses out to grass before Alvarado's judgments became public knowledge. He needed time to master his voice and the muscles around his mouth before anyone else spoke to him about Demonio.

Within the next half hour, word did come, but it was brought by a man who knew about the judgments. Alonso Rojas was being sent with a companion to reconnoiter the land through which they would travel when they marched again. After saddling his horse, Rojas stopped to speak.

"I am sorry about the horse, *amigo*. I had intended asking that you ride out with us today."

"*Gracias, señor.*" It would have been an honor beyond belief but a simple word of thanks was all Luis dared manage.

Between the picket line and the gates there were no more encounters, but as the horses and their attendants were passing through the gates, Luis saw that a stone had lodged itself between Demonio's hoof and shoe. He fell behind to remove it and was overtaken by a burial party led by Fray Francisco Martinez de Pontaza, the thinner of the two Franciscan friars, the one with the wispy beard.

Separated from the others, Luis crossed himself and followed at a respectful distance. The party stopped before the grazing land was reached and he was obliged to stop also.

Mass having been said inside the city, now all that remained was to place the blanket-wrapped body in an open grave.

"Lord, we pray that thou wilt show abiding mercy to the soul of Thy servant. May he rest in peace." Fray Pontaza sprinkled the holy water, earth was shoveled into the grave, and all those who had accompanied the body, except for the friar, turned back.

Luis was about to lead Demonio past him when the friar began to pray again, this time in Spanish instead of Latin.

"Our Father, I ask Thy mercy also for the soul of the hapless Indian who killed this man we have just committed to earth. He sinned less than he was sinned against."

Stunned, Luis stared with open mouth at the back of Pontaza's habit. Then Demonio whinnied and the friar turned away from the grave.

"I see my prayer shocked you," he said dryly, noticing the expression on Luis' face. "I assure you it will not displease our Heavenly Father. It must grieve Him sorely that the poor Indians are hunted and slaughtered like wild beasts by those who profess Christianity."

"But they're only savages," Luis protested. "And they have no souls. All the conquistadores say so."

"It is convenient for them to think so," the friar said bitterly. "But the Church does not agree, nor does the Crown. Why do you think our Gracious Sovereign appointed a Protector of the Indians? Or have you never heard of Fray Bartolomé de Las Casas?"

"No," Luis replied, edging away from the burning look in the friar's eyes. Then he remembered. It had been on the cliff, after the Indians guarding the ravine had been slaughtered. He *had* heard the name. "Yes, I did once," he corrected himself. "I—I heard him called crazy."

Confusion, not rudeness had prompted this reply. Immediately the words were out, Luis wished them back but it was too late.

"Crazy!" The friar's eyes blazed in such a way that Luis was frightened and he dug his fingers into Demonio's mane.

"Crazy to believe the Indians should be brought to the knowledge of our Lord through kindness and justice only!" Then Pontaza sighed and the fire left his eyes.

"Some day I want to tell you about Las Casas but now I see you wouldn't listen. Your thoughts are on something else."

He looked closely at Luis and then at Demonio. "You are the boy against whom charges were brought last night, are you not? And is this the horse?"

Luis' heart felt like a sponge suddenly squeezed. To discuss Demonio now would be more than he could bear. But Pontaza continued.

"Diego Sánchez has told me of your love for the animal. Sometimes it eases the heart to talk; come tell me about it."

Tell Pontaza! Luis only wanted to escape from him, but this time he controlled his tongue.

"I thank you, Father," he stammered. "Some other time, perhaps, but I am already delayed in taking the horse to pasture and—"

"Some other time, then." The friar dusted off the skirts of his garment and walked away.

It was dusk the next day when Rojas and his companion returned with news. Beyond the mountains large numbers of Quichés were massing. Whether to meet the Spaniards in peace or war, Rojas had been unable to learn. Perhaps the Quiché defeat at Zapotitlán had convinced them it was better to submit quietly to the rule of Spain, or perhaps because of it the Quichés were preparing to offer fiercer resistance.

"Well, we shall soon find out," Alvarado commented and ordered his officers to make ready for departure in the morning.

At sunrise he drew up his men in the market place. Standing in his stirrups on his big chestnut horse he made the troops a rousing speech.

"We have, as you know, sent the Quichés offers of our friendship," he said in loud ringing tones. "If they receive us as friends, we shall welcome them as vassals of our most mighty and worshipful king, requiring only that they pay him tribute and that they give up their idols and accept the True Faith. But," and here his voice took on added zeal, "if in wickedness they choose to fight, we must punish them."

A soldier started to cheer but Alvarado held up a hand to quiet him.

"We will defeat them no matter how great their number. We will slaughter as we must but take all the slaves we need. When we reach their cities we shall smash their idols and empty their storehouses. Thus far there has been too little gold to divide. Ahead there is enough to make every man in this army rich for life. Each man will have slaves to carry his share and it will be so heavy that they will stagger under it."

Alvarado's expression kindled the same look of greed in other faces. It was as though the men could already see the storehouses filled with gold and precious jewels.

Again a cheer was started and this time Alvarado made no attempt to quiet it. It rang out, filling every corner of the market place. Carried away, Luis started to join in; then his throat closed and he looked in another direction. His eyes fell on the thin ascetic features and wispy beard of Pontaza. On the friar's face, naked for all to see, was condemnation.

Luis drew his eyes back quickly. Bitter as he felt against

Alvarado, he had no desire to ally himself with Fray Pontaza. If the enemy wouldn't submit, clearly they should be punished. It wasn't sensible to think otherwise.

When the cheering died away, the army moved out in its accustomed formation. The metal helmets of the conquistadores reflected the sun. The bright feathers in the headdresses of the Mexican and Tlascalan chieftains bobbed and swayed with each step. It was a scene that had been repeated many times since leaving Mexico and always before it had caused Luis' heart to leap. It beat faster now also, but his foremost feeling was one of relief to be on the move again, and leaving the place where he'd received such hurt.

For half a league beyond Zapotitlán the route over which they traveled was a bloody shambles. Earth had been thrown over the bodies pitched out of the city, but no such effort had been made here. Luis noticed that the face of Doña Luisa was pale and that beads of sweat stood out on her brow. The horses too were bothered by the smell of blood, and shied as though they were seeing ghosts.

Where pursuit of the fleeing people of Zapotitlán had ceased, the beaten path lay through clean grassland again. Soldiers in the rear guard began to sing. The one who was good at setting words to familiar tunes made up a ballad about what lay before them.

"We will have more gold than we can carry."
"Gold - Gold - Gold - Gold." Those near him sang in time to their marching feet.

"So we each shall have a hundred slaves."

"Crack - crack - crack - crack." Voices imitated the sound of whips.

"The chieftains will give us their beautiful daughters."

"Ah - ah - ah - ah!"

"To our Captain will go the fairest of all."

"Ah - ah - ah - ah!"

Dismayed, Luis looked at Doña Luisa. Catching his eye, she motioned him near.

"It is only a song, *niño*," she said, smiling, "and a compliment to Tonatiuh." Then she spoke more seriously. "I hope you have not failed to take the medicine made from bark. It is not safe to leave off until we reach high ground."

"I have taken it, Doña Luisa. Bartolomé has seen to that."

"And your back, *niño?* I have heard of your punishment."

"The beating was nothing. But my shame for leaving you when there was danger is great."

"Do not distress yourself, *niño*. To be young is to be impetuous. The punishment was necessary but Tonatiuh was much pleased by your courage."

Luis' eyes went to the ground. Only yesterday these words would have caused his spirits to soar to heaven.

By midmorning they came to a narrow gorge in the Sierra Madre mountains and from there on, the way was rough. After crossing two rivers they began an ascent of incredible difficulty. The climb was so steep that the horses plunged and reared and some fell over backward. The slaves of Echeverria climbed on their hands and knees.

There was no more singing now. Just to breathe the thin high air was hard. More and more often halts were called. Then sweat turned cold and the men shivered. It was impossible to see what was happening ahead, but during one halt a wild-eyed soldier came crashing down the mountain, crying that devils were causing lightning and whirlwinds and turning men into wild beasts.

Before dark, the order came to stop for the night. There was no spot level enough to be comfortable even if the biting cold had allowed it. Keeping a tight hold on Demonio's halter rope, Luis braced himself against a tree. There had been no sign of the enemy all day but fear of an attack in a place so unfavorable to the Spaniards was in the mind of every soldier.

Bartolomé had another fear as well. Finding a place beside Luis he said, "The teats of Mamacita are dripping. Let us pray she does not foal until these hardships are past."

chapter

10

AFTER A COLD AND UNCOMFORTABLE NIGHT, MEN AND horses alike were stiff as they set out the next morning. Each hour the footing became rougher and the pass more steep and narrow. Crags too sheer for the horses to climb rose on both sides and the fallen trunks of pines lay often in their way. If the Quichés so chose, it was a perfect place for ambush.

Even those men who had been most eager for battle, and the excuse it would give for plundering, began to waver in their enthusiasm.

"I, for one, am beginning to hope the Quichés have decided not to fight," Diego Sánchez wheezed as they struggled upward.

Luis drew in a gulp of cold, thin, pine-scented air. He agreed with the blacksmith, but to say so would mean an extra breath and this he begrudged. Besides, Demonio and Mamacita were requiring all of his attention. To keep them on their feet at all was difficult as loose stones slid away from under their hoofs. He had both horses to lead now because the mule of Doña Luisa had turned balky and Bartolomé was needed to coax it from the front while the princess's servant beat it from behind.

Hidden by trees and turns in the pass, the main part of the army and also the rear guard were out of sight. It was almost as though they didn't exist, Luis thought, and the relay animals and the baggage carriers were traveling alone.

He stumbled, and in falling dragged on Mamacita's halter rope, bringing her also to her knees.

"I am sorry, little mother," he apologized when they had regained their feet. "God grant my clumsiness will not bring on your foal."

The sides of the mare were heaving and streaked with sweat, and those of Demonio also. Every time a halt was called, their blowing had a harsher rasp.

Thoughts of gold had long since left Luis' mind. For the sake of the horses, and of Doña Luisa, he prayed that the Quichés had decided to submit peacefully. Otherwise they would surely attack while the animals were still in the pass. Strung out in the bottom of the narrow defile, nothing could save them if arrows rained down from above.

By the time the sun was high, all the horses were stumbling with weariness and the Indian baggage carriers were gasping as loud as the Negro slaves of Echeverria. But still no attack had come, and beneath his exhaustion Luis began to feel reassured.

"Halt." The word was passed back from those in front.

"Halt." Luis turned and gave it to those behind. It took all his remaining breath to make his voice loud enough to carry, but no matter. There would be time now to rest.

After a minute, when the thumping of his heart quieted, he tore some grass from crevices in the rocks and offered it to Demonio and Mamacita, stroking their sweaty necks as they munched it, and giving them words of encouragement. Then he went forward to see how Doña Luisa had withstood the grueling climb. She had dismounted from her mule and sat on the ground, eyes closed and teeth clamped on her lower lip. Luis was alarmed by her pallor.

"Is she sick?" he asked Bartolomé in a whisper. "Is the child coming?"

Bartolomé shook his head and swung his arm in an arc to the right. Following its direction, Luis' eyes were caught by a flash of ruby and iridescent blue-green in the branches of a pine. The next moment a bird took flight, incredibly long and graceful emerald tail plumes streaming out behind its body. It was a bird Luis didn't know and more beautiful than any he had ever imagined. All the hardships of the climb were forgotten and even concern for Doña Luisa. The moment was one of pure delight; one that lifted the spirit and made his body feel as light and free as the bird itself.

"Oh, Bartolomé, what kind is it?" he cried when the bird had disappeared.

"Quetzal," the Tlascalan said gruffly. "But it wasn't the bird I meant. Look." He pointed again and this time Luis followed the gesture to the ground. Half blinded by the sky's brightness, at first he saw nothing. Then, as his eyes adjusted, the exaltation he'd felt drained out of him and a terrible coldness took its place.

Only a few feet away Fray Pontaza knelt in a gully. Beside him was an Indian woman, a gaping cavity in her breast where the heart should have been. At her feet lay a round fat dog cut in quarters.

Luis stared in horror. "Is she one of our friendly Indians?" he asked when he could speak.

"She is a Quiché, sacrificed by her own people," Bartolomé said. "An interpreter told Fray Pontaza. It is a sign of defiance; it means war."

"Her own people! And the poor dog also!" Luis wanted to draw his eyes away from the horrible sight but he was not able to. Nor could he move.

The mule of Doña Luisa was snorting and blowing. Above the sound of it he could hear the droning voice of Pontaza. Not all of his words but enough. He was praying for the soul of the woman and for the souls of those who had sacrificed her.

It was too much. How could the friar still believe these savages had souls? Luis began to tremble so he could scarcely control himself. Well, *por Dios*, he didn't share that belief! Anger, both at the friar and the Quiché savages, burst into a blazing flame. He ached with desire to trample and kill so many infidels that Fray Pontaza could not pray for a hundredth of them, and at the same time he was filled with the bitter realization that without a horse to ride, he'd have no opportunity.

When the order came to resume march, there was not

a man in Alvarado's army who didn't know that some-where ahead the Quichés were waiting to fall on them. The only question was when and where the attack would come. The line of march was rearranged. For the ex-hausted horses to maneuver in such terrain would be im-possible, so the cavalry dropped back and archers and infantry took the lead. The rear guard came forward as far as they could and some even marched beside the horses and baggage. High up in the hills above the pass, scouts struggled over fallen timber and deep pits left by uptorn roots, trying to keep pace with the column.

When the relay horses had moved forward the length of two gunshots, Luis saw that the last halt hadn't been for rest alone, as he'd supposed. In a place where the defile had narrowed so that only a few could march abreast, a stone barricade had been raised by the Quichés. Through this it had been necessary to make an opening before the army could advance farther.

"*Caramba!* What a spot that would have been for ambush!" A soldier of the rear guard blew on his hands to warm them. "I wonder why they have waited so long?"

He had hardly spoken when loud cries and howls broke out ahead. Luis couldn't see what was happening but knew it could only be the expected attack. Taking his obsidian-edged spear from the strap on Demonio's back, he urged him and Mamacita closer to the mule of Doña Luisa.

Again the column halted. They were at the top of the pass now and an icy wind whistled through their cloth-ing. A soldier scrambled up into a tall pine from where he could see the main body of the army descending the mountain.

"*Nombre de Dios!*" he called down. "The savages, three thousand of them at least, have struck at our allies. They are scattering them in terrible confusion."

Then a little later. "The crossbowmen have come to their support."

And again. "Alvarado is there rallying them. The Quiché savages are being driven back, but they are still taking lives."

Not since she'd remounted her mule had Doña Luisa spoken but Luis saw her lips move in prayer.

The column moved forward. As it descended the mountain, the noise of battle ahead was so loud that all other sounds were lost in it.

Suddenly Demonio snorted and reared. Luis, holding the halter rope short, was dragged upward and his startled eyes met those of an Indian high above him on a ledge overlooking the pass. The man, knife in his teeth, was already poised to leap. Luis' feet had scarcely regained the ground when the savage came hurtling through the air toward Doña Luisa.

Luis only had time to raise his spear and bound forward. There was an impact that nearly broke his wrist, and he cried out in pain as the weapon dropped from his hand. But it had done its work. On the ground, between Demonio and the mule, both snorting with fright, lay the Indian pierced through, lips drawn back in a horrible grimace. On his cheek was the letter G for *guerra*, war, which Alvarado had ordered burned there. It was

the spy who had tried to steal Mamacita and who had escaped while the army was struggling through the jungle.

Bartolomé leaned over the man and drew out the spear, and the next minute the body was trampled underfoot by the horses that followed. Luis was shaking with excitement and exhaustion as he went on, but he didn't feel sick as he had the first time he'd killed. And he was fiercely glad that Fray Pontaza had been well ahead. This soulless savage, at least, would get no prayers. As for himself, he needed no mercy for the killing; even the thought angered him.

"*Niño*," the soft voice of Doña Luisa cut into his thoughts and he realized it wasn't the first time she had tried for his attention. Her voice had come to his ears before but had gone no further. Now he looked up.

"Your pardon, Doña Luisa. I was angry and I didn't hear."

"I wanted to thank you for serving me so well. I shall not forget, nor shall Tonatiuh."

Alvarado! He didn't want Alvarado's gratitude. All he wanted from Alvarado was justice and the return of his horse. Luis turned away so Doña Luisa couldn't read his eyes.

"But why be angry at what happened, *niño?*" she asked, continuing. "To the man who tried to kill me, we are enemies. And his act was a brave one. May the Lord have mercy on his soul."

"You can't believe these infidels have souls!" Luis cried out in protest. "Not after seeing that woman who was sacrificed!"

"But I do, *niño*," she said earnestly. "The sacrifice was horrible but until the Quichés know our gentle Saviour, how can we blame them for acting as their own gods command? Before conversion, I, too, served the gods of my people."

Luis didn't answer. He couldn't. His mind was a whirl of confusion. That Doña Luisa could feel in such a way was beyond belief.

At this moment a scout, breathing hard, scrambled down the rocks and came between them.

"The Lord be praised no harm has come to you, *señora!*" he exclaimed. "Had you been killed, the fault would have been mine. I failed to see the savage until he jumped."

"Do not blame yourself," she said kindly, "but I was indeed fortunate this brave youth was at my side to protect me."

"I saw. It was an act of valor worthy of a man." The soldier gave Luis a hearty clap on the shoulder. "Well done, *compañero*."

Luis reddened with pleasure at these words of praise. *Por Dios*, it *had* been an act of valor and, as the soldier said, worthy of a man. He *was* a man!"

"Tell me, *compañero*"—Luis had never addressed a soldier as comrade before but now he felt emboldened—"tell me, was the savage alone?"

"No, there were others but as soon as he leapt, they turned and ran, even before they saw me."

"You are sure it was before?" Luis' breath quickened.

"*Seguro, compañero*." The scout smiled as he used the

word again. Then he spoke to Doña Luisa. "With your permission, *señora*, I go back above and God grant my eyes are sharper in the future."

Before, the scout had said. The other savages had taken to their heels *before* they'd seen him. This could only mean one thing, Luis knew, and on it victory might hinge. It was sight of the horses, not the scout, that had terrified them, and without doubt, Demonio's snorts and rears had added to their panic. To all but the man who had jumped, the horses were still gods. And given a chance in battle, they would run from them.

Luis was sure now that a horse, not Doña Luisa, had been the spy's target. The spy had been ordered to steal a horse in Soconusco and had failed. This time he'd been ordered to kill one so his companions could see it bleed, and carry the news back to those who waited for the cavalry to come out of the pass. He had died in the attempt. There would be no further chance for him to prove the terrible four-legged gods were only mortal animals.

When the next halt came, Luis shared his gourd of water with the two horses in his care, giving the last drops to Demonio.

"We have a right to be proud, you and I, *amigo*," he told him. "Though we march in the rear, we struck a vital blow today for Spain and the King."

Demonio, finished with drinking, placed his wet muzzle on Luis' shoulder, and so they set off on the last quarter league of descent to the plateau.

chapter

🔲🔲🔲🔲🔲🔲🔲🔲

11

THE BATTLE THAT HAD STARTED WITH THE ATTACK ON the Indian allies high up in the sierras continued all the way down the slopes. Though Luis couldn't see what was occurring, the noise of it was always ahead. It was becoming easier to breathe now, and with a sudden snap something happened inside his ears. The bitter cold of the mountain tops was left behind and a brisk, invigorating coolness took its place. The defile widened and straightened as it descended. Instead of seeing only the rumps and tails of the animals in front of him, Luis found himself looking over their heads.

The long ears of Doña Luisa's mule stood straight and alert, and the animal needed no more beating to keep it moving. It was while looking at its ears that, framed between them, Luis caught his first glimpse of the plateau below. It was broad and flat, and far ahead there was the shimmer of water crossing it. Nearer, though still at a distance, there appeared to be a large settlement on a rise of ground. Behind and on all sides of the plateau were more mountains.

"Look, *amigo*"—Bartolomé was at Luis' side, again leading Mamacita—"the vanguard is already coming out on the plain."

The infantrymen looked the size of cockroaches, and so did the Indians still fleeing from them.

Luis' hand sought Demonio's muzzle as he gazed ahead and down. "Grass, Demonio. Do you see it too? Soon you can eat your fill."

"Perhaps," Bartolomé grunted. "But perhaps there will be no time for grazing. In the distance something moves toward us."

Luis saw nothing. He stared so hard without blinking that tears stung his eyes. He looked away and then back but still he saw nothing.

"You imagine, Bartolomé," he said.

The infantry was now forming in ranks on the plain but it was not advancing. Only a small contingent of allies was still in pursuit. Soon it gave up the chase and returned. The first line of cavalry joined those on the plateau.

"Of course there will be time to graze. It is to give time that the army waits," Luis said with authority.

"Can you really not see, *amigo?*" Bartolomé asked. "It is nearer now, the moving line. Color even shows and it is that of feathers."

Luis was loath to admit that a Tlascalan's sight was keener than his own, but in another moment he, too, saw color and motion. It was coming fast, that line, drawn up in ranks like those of a civilized army. On the last slope of the mountain the boys had a view as good as though they were in an amphitheater and what was happening below, a play.

The cavalry was all on the level ground now, but still Alvarado waited while the enemy approached in unending ranks.

"*Madre de Dios!*" Diego Sánchez exclaimed. "There must be thirty thousand at least. Thirty thousand against four hundred Spaniards!"

"You forget the Tlascalans," Bartolomé said with dignity.

"Your pardon, Bartolomé. They are brave fighters and so are our other allies."

Now a howling and screaming began and arrows were launched by the Quichés.

"Why doesn't Alvarado move? Are his feet stuck to the ground?" Luis cried in a frenzy of impatience.

"Tonatiuh knows what he does," Bartolomé replied, never taking his eyes off the scene.

"And the cavalry, there is not a man mounted!" Luis continued his complaint.

A number of auxiliaries went forward to meet the advancing line and a brisk exchange of arrows took place. Then when Luis was certain the Spaniards would never move, a bugle blared. In an instant the cavalrymen mounted. The infantry opened out in front of them and the horses charged through.

As though stunned at the sight, the front ranks of the enemy halted abruptly. Many were crushed under the pounding hoofs and the rest scattered. Those in the ranks behind were no more brave. They ran as though pursued by angry gods.

Luis couldn't help laughing. He had been right. The savages did still think the horses were gods.

When the enemy had retreated, Alvarado waited until all his followers had assembled on the plateau and then he led them to some springs a league away. Since morning the horses had been without water and most of the men had long since exhausted the supplies they carried. No more could be asked of man or beast until their thirst was quenched.

The springs were so high that they were more like fountains, bubbling up out of the ground and making a large shallow pool around them. Alvarado gave leave to break ranks, and the soldiers rushed forward and threw themselves on the ground to drink. When they had finished, the horses and their attendants took their place. Luis' throat ached with dryness as he waited his turn, but at last it came. As he was leading Demonio forward, a guard gave warning. "They are coming at us again."

At the water's edge, Alvarado, helmet off and damp blond hair catching the late afternoon sun, was talking with Doña Luisa and his brother Jorge.

Luis' heart jumped into his mouth at the warning but Alvarado seemed to pay no attention.

"They are coming close." The guard ran up to him.

Alvarado looked at the man. "As I have already noticed," he said. "But until every man and horse has had enough, we will not move."

"But, Excellency, they can surround us; they outnumber us more than thirty times."

"And what of it?" Alvarado asked. His voice was cool but his eyes shone and his teeth flashed in a brilliant smile.

"He enjoys making a game of danger; it is arrogance,"

Luis told himself, knowing that less than a week before he would have hailed it as courage.

"Another drink, anyone?" Alvarado looked around him, his voice maddeningly calm. "No? Well, then, let us at them again."

He bowed to Doña Luisa. "*Adiós, querida mia;* it shall be as you ask." To his brother Jorge he spoke crisply but without hurry. "The baggage and relay horses will remain here with you. The cannon also. We will return and camp at the springs tonight."

He gave the order to re-form ranks. As the bugle sounded it, the men milling around the water's edge went back to their companies and those officers who owned relay animals mounted them. Alvarado had already changed to his chestnut from the slow but sure-footed dun he had ridden across the mountains.

Until the attacking party was close enough for even those in the rear to see the skins of wild beasts in which they were clothed, Alvarado held his men. In the head-dress of the leader Luis noticed plumes of emerald green, like those of the bird he had seen high up in the sierras.

"It is the prince Ahzumanche," word was passed back.

When at last Alvarado moved out to meet the prince, the two forces were scarcely more than a bowshot apart. As before, arrows flew through the air, but now Luis and Bartolomé were near enough to hear the whistle. The clash of spears against steel and the screams and shouts were almost deafening. Then again the enemy retreated, but this time Alvarado pursued.

"Ahzumanche . . ." Luis turned to Bartolomé when the

sound of battle faded into the distance. "You remember what the man who tried to steal Mamacita said? He said he had come with the prince Ahzumanche."

"I remember," Bartolomé replied. "It was Ahzumanche who spoke with the voice of an owl. I noticed that he looked boldly at the horses as he advanced just now. As though not afraid of them. I think he may not be running from our army but leading it."

Now that Bartolomé had pointed this out, Luis agreed it was possible. It was a worrying thought, but soon a more immediate worry took its place. Ever since she had drunk at the springs, Mamacita had been acting with unaccustomed restlessness. She would lie down and get up, only to lie down again. She had done this more than a dozen times, breaking out into sweat, though the air was cool. Suddenly water gushed from her.

"She foals!" Bartolomé exclaimed in dismay. "I must find Señor Sánchez quickly!"

Sánchez, who a few minutes earlier had been nearby, wasn't in sight. Bartolomé set out to find him but returned alone.

Mamacita now lay on her side with all four legs stretched out and breathing hard. She was surrounded by Mexicans and Tlascalans, looking on with curiosity and jabbering in their own tongues.

"Ask if any have ever delivered a foal," Luis told Bartolomé. Bartolomé repeated the question in both languages but the answer was No.

"Then find someone who has. Anyone. No, wait. It is too late. You may have to help me."

"You, Luis? Have you done this thing before?" Bartolomé sounded frightened.

"No, but I have been with my father when he has. Look, already the front legs and nose push through."

Bartolomé dropped to his knees beside Luis at the rear of the mare. "It comes in a sack!" he said in wonder.

"Of course."

Now the shoulders showed and Luis gave a gentle pull. Mamacita grunted and the body slipped out. Then Luis waited until the hips appeared before pulling again.

"So." It was the voice of Diego Sánchez.

Luis looked up, sweat dripping from his forehead into his eyes. "*Señor*, I am glad you are here," he said with relief. "As you can see, Mamacita is foaling."

"She has foaled," the big man laughed. Luis looked down at the mare again. There on the ground, complete and freed from the sack, lay a small wet foal.

Sánchez took over then, sending Luis for warm water and a handful of pounded meal for gruel. When he returned, the afterbirth had dropped and he helped Bartolomé to clear it away and bring clean grass for the foal to lie on.

As darkness began to fall, the cavalry returned with a clatter, followed a little later by the infantry. Fires were lit and dried meat thrown in the stew pots. Alonso Rojas came up to Luis and put an arm across his shoulder.

"I hear you've been midwife to a filly, and a good one too," he said, "but I wish you could have been with us. What a day we had!"

"Tell me, *señor*," Luis begged eagerly. "Was it as Bartolomé supposed? Was Ahzumanche leading you to a place more favorable for the Quichés to fight?"

"He was indeed," Rojas laughed. "But more than one can play at that game. He led us to a mountain where a vast number of savages were hidden. It was there he wanted to fight us but our Captain outfoxed him. He pretended fear and turned the horses back toward the springs."

"What then?" Luis' excitement was mounting.

"Patience, boy. I come to that. Well then, seeing the horses in what they supposed was flight, the savages took heart. Their fear of the animals lessened and they came after them, urged on by Ahzumanche. Alvarado let them reach the horses' tails well out on open ground before we turned on them. *Por Dios*, what punishment we gave. Hundreds were killed, Ahzumanche among them." Rojas sighed. "A brave man, that one. Had he been born a Spaniard I would have been proud to call him friend."

As soon as they had eaten, the men who had fought all day fell into exhausted sleep. Only the guards and Diego Sánchez remained awake. Opening his eyes once or twice during the night, Luis saw the blacksmith feeding more warm gruel to Mamacita or rubbing grease into the wounds of the horses that had been injured that afternoon.

Too soon the sun rose. Luis yawned, stretched, and got up from the ground to lead Demonio to water. Returning, he stopped to visit Mamacita. The foal was standing on wobbly legs, nursing. She was a scrawny little thing for so

large a mother, but a pretty chestnut color. She lost the
teat and butted angrily against the bag and then turned
to stare at Luis from large dark eyes. His heart grew
warm as he looked at her.

"Has she a name yet, Señor Sánchez?" he asked.

The smith shook his head. "Have you one in mind?"

"Yes. Once I had a chestnut filly. Her name was Preciosa. Do you think she could be called that?"

"And why not?" Sánchez smiled. "She is yours, *chico*."

"Mine? She's mine?" Luis was dazed with wonder and
happiness. Already love for the little animal possessed
him.

"She is yours right enough," the smith assured him.
"The Captain ordered it so."

Alvarado! Luis drew his eyes away from the foal and
looked at the ground; disappointment had hit him like a
blow in the groin. From Alvarado he would take nothing.

"I cannot accept her." He spoke stiffly.

"As you wish." Sánchez's voice was also stiff. "She will
need carrying when we move out this morning, if she is
not to be left behind. Perhaps you are right. The burden
would be great."

In the sky vultures circled. Vultures always followed the
path of battle. Luis was used to the sight of them. Still,
he shivered.

"You wouldn't leave her behind!"

Sánchez let him wait for a reply while he, too, looked
up at the vultures. "No," he said at last. "But a carrier
must be found. One I can trust to treat her gently, not
like a sack of dried meat."

Luis' eyes went again to Preciosa. She had finished nursing and lay stretched flat on the grass. To carry such a little one like a sack of dried meat! Already Luis felt indignant at the carrier. No, it mustn't be like that. She needed love and much care.

"It isn't because of the burden I refuse," he said. "I shall carry her anyway."

"Then why, *chico?*" Sánchez looked both relieved and puzzled.

"It is something I do not wish to talk about."

"Then it is none of my affair. But just the same let me give you a bit of advice. Don't refuse her too hastily. Once a thing is said, it is often too late to change the mind."

It was already too late. Already he had told Alvarado at Zapotitlán that he would accept nothing but Demonio from him. But this Luis didn't say to Diego Sánchez.

chapter
🝖🝖🝖🝖🝖🝖🝖🝖
12

FOR TWO DAYS THE ARMY HAD LIVED ON WHAT IT CARRIED. Behind it lay the grueling journey over the mountains from the lowlands of the Pacific. Ahead lay the capitals of the three main kingdoms that shared the highlands of Guatemala.

Before marching against Utatlán, the Quiché capital, Alvarado decided his men needed rest and food. A league from the springs was the city they'd seen from the mountain tops—Quezaltenango, the second largest in the Quiché kingdom. But after the punishment its people had received, Alvarado anticipated little trouble in persuading its chieftains to play hosts to his tired and hungry army.

The journey was an easy one for everyone except Luis and, as it turned out, Bartolomé. In spite of her small size, the foal was a heavy burden and there was no convenient way to carry her. She could not be slung on the back as the baggage was, supported by thongs tied to a strap on the forehead. Luis had to hold her in front, one arm under her chest and one under her rump, with her legs hanging down and bumping his knees at every step. To make matters worse, she would suddenly let out small squeals and struggle to get loose. Ten minutes at a time was all Luis could manage. Then Bartolomé would take her while Luis led Demonio and Mamacita. After another ten minutes Luis would carry her again and Bartolomé lead the horses.

Not even in the jungle or ascending the mountain had a journey seemed so long. Because ten minutes seemed an hour, the city never appeared to grow any nearer. At last, though, they began to travel through orchards and cultivated fields and they could see houses and temples on the rise ahead.

The main army had already been inside the gates for some minutes when Luis staggered up the incline. As he followed the baggage carriers and relay horses into the central square, he was nearly at the end of his endurance. With a great sigh of relief, Luis set Preciosa down beside her mother, where she promptly fell to nursing while he leaned against a building for support.

At first, exhausted, he noticed nothing strange about the city. Then gradually he became aware that the only faces in the square were familiar ones and that except for a few round-bellied little dogs, the streets running off from it were empty. In the courtyard of the house against which he stood, he could hear a fountain tinkling but in the house itself there were no sounds.

"What is wrong do you think, Bartolomé?" he asked.

"Hush, Tonatiuh is about to speak."

Alvarado, who had dismounted, was helped back into the

saddle. He looked down at the men surrounding him.

"Well, gentlemen," he said with a wry smile, "it seems our hosts didn't stay to greet us. I will send out messengers to bring them back, but in the meantime let us enjoy the food they left behind. As you saw when we passed through, there is plenty more in the fields and orchards.

"The army, except for a strong guard, will be quartered here in the city. The baggage will remain here also. The horses will return to the plains outside and a camp will be established there under the command of Jorge Alvarado. While we wait, let us eat and rest. God knows we need to do both."

After the boys had taken the horses back to the plain, Bartolomé returned to the city. When he joined Luis again he had the news of the market place.

"Tonatiuh has already sent out the messengers. They are to promise kind treatment if the inhabitants will return and become loyal vassals of the King—giving tribute, of course. The messengers are to say Tonatiuh knows it was the Quichés of Utatlán who were to blame for the battles and for leading the people of Quezaltenango against us."

"Is it thought that they will come back?"

Bartolomé shrugged.

"What else then?" Sometimes Bartolomé pretended he wasn't much interested in news but he always liked to have it pulled out of him.

"The soldiers have searched all the houses and temples. Even in the temple of Tohil there is not one piece of gold or ornament left."

"Is Alvarado angry?"

Bartolomé gave another shrug. "Of course, but he told the soldiers again about the treasures of Utatlán."

Quezaltenango was too large and important a place to leave without pacifying its people, so the army settled down to await their return. The rest was welcome, the food abundant, and the climate healthy. Those who had contracted the ague in the swamps no longer suffered from chills and fever. As for the land, it was the most beautiful and luxuriant the Spaniards had ever seen, and after the dashing torrents of the mountains its many streams seemed like smooth shining ribbons. Even the great volcanic peak that dominated the landscape close to the city appeared friendly as it sent lazily drifting clouds of steam into the bluest of skies.

But none of this affected Luis. Each morning when he woke his first thought was of Preciosa. He must go to Alvarado. He must tell the Captain that he refused to accept the foal. Then every day, after all, he put it off until the next.

"Tomorrow I shall go," he told himself each night before he slept, but always he dreamed of ways that would make it possible for him to keep Preciosa.

While the army waited, many stories began to circulate throughout the camp. The chieftains had refused Alvarado's offer of friendship; they would not return. The chieftains had accepted his offer; they would return soon and make peace. One story persisted. If peace could be made, a Spanish mission would be built between Quezaltenango and the mountains, in the area called Zacaha. When this rumor was established as fact, a few soldiers began to talk of joining this small colony. Gold so far had been only a promise, but the land was rich, and colonization and propagation of the Holy Faith were both duties of the expedition as set forth in its charter.

For Luis the idea held little appeal, especially when he learned that the priest who would serve the colony was to be Fray Pontaza.

One evening Pontaza spoke to a group of men gathered around a cooking fire. Luis, who was one of this group, had no choice but to listen.

"Through kindness and upright example we shall win the natives of this place for God," the friar said, his eyes burning with enthusiasm in his pale, bearded face. "We shall live as brothers with them. There shall be no forced labor and no demands for gold. We will be guided by the ideals that Las Casas, Protector of the Indians, strove for in his colony at Cumaná on the north coast of Tierra Firme."

Until the fire grew low, Pontaza's impassioned voice went on telling of Las Casas' plan, whereby Spaniard and Indian would work side by side and confidence would be established by lack of weapons of any kind.

Out of respect there could be no interruption, but once when Pontaza paused for breath a soldier asked dryly, "And wasn't this colony at Cumaná wiped out by the savages?"

"That is true," the friar admitted, "but only because the Spaniards already in the area opposed Las Casas and the authority given him by the King. When Las Casas left to protest this interference and bring back help, the man he put in charge of the colony betrayed him. He took gold and pearls from the natives and made them slaves."

The soldiers were becoming restless. Was Alvarado as mad as the friar to think such a colony as Pontaza proposed could exist one week after the main army moved on?

"Does Pedro Alvarado know of these plans?" a voice on the other side of the fire asked.

"He leaves it to me to make these people our friends. To me and de Leon Cardona."

"Captain Cardona, eh?" It was Sánchez who spoke now. "A good officer. Has he agreed to use no arms?"

"He has not agreed to remain without them. But it is his opinion that not even God could save us if we used them. We will be only a handful of Spaniards in a community of ten thousand Indians."

At length Pontaza left. There had not been many in the group around the fire who had considered joining the colony when he'd started speaking. Now there were none.

Luis had sat stiff and uncomfortable throughout the entire visit. Whenever he'd looked up he'd found Pontaza's eyes fastened on him, and when he looked at the ground he could still feel them. It was as though the friar were trying to hypnotize him, willing him to volunteer for the colony.

Even if the good-humored and understanding Father Godinez were to be the priest instead of Pontaza, Luis wouldn't have volunteered. His skin rose in goose pimples at the thought of it. To face death fighting next to brave companions was one thing. To face death without lifting a hand, no matter how great one's trust in God, was another. This took a different kind of courage and it was not his kind. Luis didn't feel ashamed that this was so, but a grudging feeling of admiration for Pontaza began to grow in him.

As time passed and the people of Quezaltenango did not return, the army became impatient. With stomachs full and bodies rested, the promise of gold and jewels at Utatlán beckoned more strongly every day. Some men grumbled out loud, saying it was folly to wait longer, but still Alvarado didn't move.

It seemed to Luis that he and Pontaza were the only ones who weren't burning with eagerness to press on. The friar was loath to leave while there was still hope, of the natives returning and making peace, because otherwise no colony would be established. Luis' reason for welcoming delay was the filly. She must be able to run by herself before they moved again.

Every day they waited she grew stronger. She frisked and bucked as she circled around Mamacita, begging her to play, and sometimes she even wandered off among the other horses until her mother's worried nicker brought her back.

On the morning of the sixth day, after he had watered Demonio and brushed him until his coat shone, Luis stood watching Preciosa nurse, her stiff little tail flicking this way and that. He was, as usual, in an unhappy state about her. A hundred times he'd said to himself what he'd said to Alvarado right after the court at Zapotitlán. If he couldn't have Demonio, he would accept nothing else from him. And yet he wanted to keep the foal most terribly. She tugged at his heart as strongly as she was tugging at her mother's teats.

Luis still hadn't been able to bring himself to approach Alvarado but he knew he must before they left Quezaltenango. He must thank him for offering the gift and refuse it as politely as possible. He couldn't accept Preciosa, no matter how much he wanted her. Nothing had changed since Zapotitlán. There was no sense in delaying an action that grew harder every day. He might better get it over with.

Luis climbed the steep rise to the city. From Alvarado's headquarters came loud boisterous voices and laughter. Whatever was going on couldn't be interrupted. Feeling he'd been granted a reprieve, he was about to go back to the camp when Alvarado came out. He was alone and he stopped. It had to be now after all.

"Excellency," Luis began. He swallowed and began again. "Excellency—"

"Well?" Alvarado asked. Then, abruptly, he held up his hand for silence. From the direction of the wall a sentry was calling out. They couldn't hear his words but in a moment a guard came running up.

"They come!" he shouted. "The people of Quezaltenango are returning."

Alvarado strode off after the guard and Luis followed close at their heels. The market place had suddenly filled with soldiers, all running toward the spot from which the returning inhabitants had been seen. In the middle of a jostling crowd Luis was brought up short. Just in front of him was the only person who was not running. It was

Fray Pontaza. He was on his knees and seemed oblivious to the danger of trampling feet. Luis longed to rush on but he couldn't; the friar might be hurt if left unguarded. So he braced himself and received the heedless buffeting of those behind, in Pontaza's stead. When they had passed on, the friar rose as calmly as though he had been praying in the safety of a church.

"My son, is it not wonderful of God to have brought this to pass!" His eyes were shining with joy. "Now that the inhabitants return to make peace, the colony is assured. Give your thanks also, my son."

Luis chafed at the delay but he couldn't well refuse. He dropped to his knees and crossed himself. "Our Heavenly Father, I thank Thee," he mumbled. Then bounding up, he was off.

The rooftops near the wall were crowded with soldiers. On one, Alvarado stood with Puertocarrero and Captain Chávez. All three were staring intently at a scene that was hidden from those on the ground.

Suddenly Alvarado turned and bellowed for silence. When the men quieted, he shouted, "We have been fooling ourselves, *compañeros*. The inhabitants are not returning in peace. There are too many by thousands and still they pour from the hills. It would seem they have been joined by every warrior in the entire Quiché nation. To arms, all!"

His eye fell on Luis who was trying to scramble up onto the next roof. "Run for the camp, boy. Apprise my brother Jorge of our danger. There is no time to lose."

chapter

🔲🔲🔲🔲🔲🔲🔲🔲

13

THE BATTLE OF QUEZALTENANGO WAS THE FIERCEST THE
Spaniards had yet fought. Tecún Umán, the general-in-
chief of the Quiché forces, had come from Utatlán to
take the field in person and he commanded warriors from
every city and town in the kingdom. Tecún Umán was as
brave as the young Ahzumanche and far more experienced.
And by now, many of the warriors he led had lost their
greatest fear of the cavalry. They had seen horses bleed
when wounded. The animals still were terrible but they
were not gods.

After setting his men in order, with the camp well
guarded and cannon facing the great plain over which
Tecún was advancing, Alvarado rode out at the head of
ninety cavalry and two hundred infantry. Ahead of him,
from far-off hills to the middle of the plain, there was
not even a small patch of ground that lay still under the
noonday sun. In the distance the ground crawled as with
millions of ants, and nearer it bristled with spears and
waved with plumes. Behind Alvarado were less than three
hundred Spaniards and yet he faced Tecún's hordes as

though he, too, were backed by tens of thousands.

From the camp Luis watched, wishing himself one of the three hundred. He saw Alvarado take up a position favorable to the cavalry and pointed this out to Bartolomé. "We were in time, *amigo*. The battle must be fought where it is best for the horses."

There had been noise in camp as well as from the battlefield. Suddenly it ceased except for a harsh whispering, as if a hundred breaths were being drawn in at the same instant.

Tecún's warriors had been advancing in the solid formation most advantageous to the Spaniards, as it left each line vulnerable in turn when the one in front was mowed down by guns or trampled by horses. Now something different was happening. Tecún's ranks separated. Vast numbers of warriors began moving out to the right and to the left. Then, when more than a gunshot apart, they swept forward at a run in two great divisions.

Those in camp could only watch in horror. When the columns converged, the small Spanish army would be trapped between them.

"No defense is possible," Bartolomé said despairingly. "We must pray Tonatiuh can retreat in time." Then a minute later, he pointed. "See, he is preparing to move back. But I think it is too late."

Luis, too, felt the situation was hopeless. Then in one bewildering and incredible moment it changed.

Alvarado was not retreating. He was attacking. He hurled his two platoons of cavalry, captained by Chávez and Puertocarrero, in a flanking movement against the division coming in on his left, and at the same time he led an infantry charge against Tecún's second division.

The onslaught was terrible. After the first few moments it was impossible for the boys to tell what was happening, so great was the confusion. Metal helmets and plunging horses appeared and disappeared in a sea of plumes. Muskets barked, arrows whined, and the air quivered with fearsome screams and yells. And still the Quichés poured in from the hills.

Then a lone horseman came spurring back into camp and halted by the relay horses. It was Rojas. An officer and some men of the rear guard ran up and surrounded him, asking for news.

"The infantry is hard pressed," he told them, fighting for breath. "Alvarado's horse is lamed. He sends for another."

Breaking away from the circle, he saw Luis standing just beyond. "Saddle Demonio," he shouted.

For a split second Luis stood still, frozen with shock. Alvarado had never yet ridden Demonio. Luis had come to believe he never intended to.

"Hurry!" Rojas' voice was rough with impatience.

The spell was broken. Luis moved fast, bringing saddle and bridle. But while his fingers worked swiftly, adjusting straps and buckles, he sobbed childishly under his breath. "He has no right! It is I and no one else who should ride Demonio in battle!"

Then, like an arrow, a thought pierced his rebellion—a thought of satisfaction. It wouldn't be for long that Alvarado rode Demonio. One jerk on the bit and the horse would come galloping loose back to camp. It would be a fine revenge for the injustice with which Alvarado had treated him!

Rojas saluted the rear guard officer. "I ask permission
for the boy to ride with me. He will be needed."

"He may go." The officer also saluted.

Luis seized his spear and vaulted into the saddle. So
at least he was to ride Demonio until they came up with
the Captain. Perhaps he would even have the good fortune of seeing the great Alvarado unseated.

They set off at full gallop. It was good to be on Demonio's back again even for so short a ride. Luis half
hoped some Quichés would spring up in their path so he
could cut them down, but they met no one until, topping a
small rise, they found Alvarado. He had dropped back
from the wildly milling action ahead. Still on his horse, he
was laying about him with a sword as four or five Indians
who had penetrated behind the Spanish line tried to pull
him off.

"*Santiago!*" Rojas yelled as they rushed forward, and
the Indians scattered.

"*Por Dios*, I am glad to see you," Alvarado exclaimed as
he came down from the saddle. "The infantry needs encouragement—and quickly. Echeverria tries to drive the
men forward without giving them heart. Besides, his animal is slow. I must relieve him before the men turn."

He laid a hand on the sweaty neck of his big chestnut.
"*Adiós*," he said, then looked approvingly at Demonio.
Demonio was dancing about at the end of the reins which
Luis, also dismounted, had looped over one arm. For the
moment Luis was paying him little attention. His eyes were
straining in the direction of the battle.

So Echeverria led the infantry until the Captain could

rejoin it. Was it imagination or was the battle actually closer than it had been a moment ago? Was it imagination that made the howling seem louder? Or was Echeverria unable to stop a retreat that might turn into a rout?

"A leg up, boy!"

Luis turned and, stepping close to Demonio's side, bent a knee and held his hands in position to cup Alvarado's boot. This was no time for revenge. The battle depended on Alvarado—and on Demonio!

Alvarado's weight almost crushed Luis into the ground but he managed to gasp, "Excellency—Demonio's mouth —more than a touch on the bit and he will fight you as he fought Captain Echeverria. A hand on the shoulder brings him up—in turning he obeys the legs."

Alvarado's face showed nothing. Had he understood? Did he resent the advice? Luis couldn't tell because even before he gathered his reins, Alvarado put the horse into a gallop.

"*Vaya con Dios*, Luis," Rojas called as he too set off.

The sound of retreating hoofs was a lonely one. Luis looked at the chestnut. It was a noble animal and plainly suffering.

"We will need God with us if we are to make camp in safety," he told him, running a gentle hand over the lathered neck.

The horse limped badly and Luis had to lead him slowly, pausing often. Each time he looked over his shoulder anxiously, fearing the Indians Rojas had scattered might show themselves. Then at last they were within a bowshot of camp and safe.

"*Santiago!*" The cry rose loud and clear above the howl of Indians.

"*Santiago!*" Luis echoed. Alvarado had his men in hand. They were attacking. There would be no retreat.

The conflict raged until sunset and climaxed at the River Olintipeque, where it flowed broad and shallow through the plains, turning it red with the blood of slaughtered Quichés. Some of the enemy escaped up a bare rocky hill, but they were pursued to the top and slaughtered also. Tecún Umán was killed during the course of the battle.

At dusk the army returned to camp, to be greeted with such cheering as Luis had never heard before. Those who had remained behind crowded around the weary troops.

"*Hola*, Juan!" and a dirt and blood-encrusted soldier would be crushed in a bearlike hug. "*Hola*, Carlos! *Hola*, Diego!"

Luis rushed up to a soldier. "Tell me, *señor*, did the black the Captain rode come safely through the battle?"

"I don't know, *chico*." Then the man was borne off by friends.

In the confusion and excitement Luis didn't see Alvarado until he was beside him, dismounting. And, yes, *gracias a Dios*, it was from Demonio!

"You trained the horse well," Alvarado said, giving him the reins. "How is the chestnut?"

Luis laid his cheek against Demonio's cheek. "Diego Sánchez says—" But the smith had come up and answered for himself.

"A blow on the shoulder causes the lameness, Excellency. He cannot be ridden for some time."

"*Qué mal fortuna.*" Alvarado let out a gusty sigh. "Then it's well the black is fast enough to take his place. He has lost a shoe, however. See to it before morning."

"We are nearly at the end of those we carry with us," Sánchez told him.

"I know. Too many lie behind us sucked down in the swamp. Well," he said with a shrug, "we will have to buy iron from Echeverria when we run out."

Alvarado strode off and Sánchez fell to cursing Echeverria. "The devil take him for a robber," he said after many oaths. "You know what he is asking for his iron? Enough to bring shoes to 190 pesos a dozen!"

Then he spat on the ground. "Well, *chico*, when you have finished cooling Demonio, bring him to the forge. At least we can be glad the Captain did not have to support your claim to the horse."

"What has that to do with it?" Luis asked, stiffening as he always did when mention was made of Alvarado's decision—a decision that still only he and the Captain knew had been lacking in honor.

"Just this. Echeverria's price would be even higher. And to the Captain and others who sided with the Captain, he might refuse to sell at all. Before too long half the horses might be traveling on bare, sore feet. And as for the fighting—"

"Alvarado leads the expedition. He gives the commands. He could take the iron," Luis broke in, in angry protest.

"Don't be a fool, boy," Sánchez growled. "The iron belongs to Echeverria. If Pedro Alvarado took it, half the army—his brother Gonzalo among them—would be against him."

So! His rights had been traded for iron. The Captain had avoided unpopularity at his expense.

As Luis rubbed Demonio dry and then led him about, cooling him, these galling thoughts stuck in his gullet. They walked the length of the field where the horses were picketed, passing Rojas' roan, Chávez' sorrel, and Puertocarrero's brown. These were all horses that Sánchez had meant when he spoke of sore feet. For a moment Luis thought of what this would mean. Then he shook the thought off.

It hadn't been necessary to rob him of Demonio to keep this from happening. Alvarado could *take* the iron. Sánchez hadn't denied this. The Captain's word was law. Why did it matter what half the army thought? Did Alvarado have to be popular with all? Did conceit demand this? Did justice count for nothing?

With every question Luis asked himself, his anger increased. Even Demonio seemed to feel the current of it through his halter rope. He broke into a second sweat. Luis used the cloth again and then led him farther.

At the end of the field they faced the great plain where the battle had taken place. Luis started to turn Demonio but instead he halted, looking out toward the hills. They were only dark shapes now against an almost dark sky. Then he saw them differently. Tecún Umán's hordes were sweeping down out of them again, dividing into two great arms trying to crush the army between them. What would have happened if half the army had been against Alvarado then? Luis didn't ask the question. It asked itself and the answer came by itself also. No one, not even a great general like Alvarado, could have led such an army to victory against so great odds.

For a while longer Luis stared at the hills, his thoughts in conflict. In taking Demonio, Alvarado had acted without honor, pretending he didn't know to whom the horse belonged. But the action had kept the army together. Except for this, every member of the expedition might have been destroyed.

He ran a hand along Demonio's flank. It felt dry and cool. "You too might now be dead, *amigo*." He sighed. "That still doesn't make what the Captain did honest, but it wasn't as I thought it, either. Well, let us return to the forge. You will get a new shoe and many other new shoes because the Captain took you from me. So will the other horses. And the army will win many more victories for the same reason."

A short distance from the forge Mamacita was tethered, Preciosa loose at her side. The foal ran up to Luis, bucking and playing, and came to a sudden stop with all four legs stiffly braced. He fondled her.

"I shall keep you after all, little one," he said. "Tomorrow I shall tell the Captain so."

In the morning Luis sought out Alvarado. He found him at headquarters. "Excellency, I have come to thank you for the gift of the filly," he said when a guard admitted him to the Captain's presence.

"And high time," Alvarado remarked dryly, but he looked amused rather than angry. "However, I have lost a wager with myself. When I took Demonio from you, you said if you couldn't have justice you would take nothing else. What has changed your mind? Do you no longer think I was unjust?"

Luis drew himself up very straight. "I have not changed my mind about the decision, Excellency. It was unjust. But it was better for the army. I know that now. I know about the iron."

Alvarado rose and clapped him on the shoulder. "Well, Luis, we agree at last," he said heartily. "For the army, the rights of any individual must be sacrificed when necessary."

"Even your rights, Excellency?"

"*Por Dios*, boy, I *am* the army. Surely you know that?" His hand dropped from Luis' shoulder but a moment later he smiled at him.

"Some day it may be possible for me to give Demonio back to you. In the meantime he serves the army well. You have made a good job of his training. Tell me, have you taught him anything beyond what you told me in the field?"

Luis hesitated. It was easy for Alvarado to make this half-promise when he knew it wouldn't be possible. Luis felt like saying so but he didn't. He answered the question only.

"Nothing that would be of use in battle, Excellency. But he bows if tickled in a certain way under the right foreleg and snorts if touched in a certain place under the barrel."

"Does he now? You must show me sometime." Alvarado

looked as pleased as a small boy.

"Excellency." A guard was at the door.

"Do not interrupt," Alvarado ordered curtly.

"But, Excellency, four chieftains of Quezaltenango have returned from the hills. They are outside with Father Godinez and Fray Pontaza."

"Well, why didn't you say so?" Alvarado snapped. "Bring them to me at once."

When the guard left on his errand, Alvarado spoke to Luis again. "It was Doña Luisa who asked me to give you the filly. You must thank her also."

If, in time, Alvarado found reason for taking Preciosa as he'd taken Demonio, Luis was certain that he'd do so. But there mightn't be a reason. He would pray that there would not be.

"I shall thank her, Excellency. I am grateful to you both."

On his way out of the building Luis passed the party coming in. The chieftains were imposing-looking men, splendid in long feather-embroidered cloaks with brilliant green quetzal plumes in their headdresses and gold ornaments in their noses and ears. They were accompanied by Godinez, Pontaza, and an interpreter. Pontaza's eyes were gleaming with fervor as, through the interpreter, he kept up a steady flow of conversation. He had grasped at the opportunity to begin telling of the Saviour.

The next days were busy. After receiving the chieftains and hearing of their wish to become loyal vassals of Spain, Alvarado entertained them at dinner with all dignity. In the morning he gave them Spanish cloaks and

swords and sent them out to assure their people of his friendship and to ask them to come back. They returned in droves, and hundreds were baptized.

To Luis' surprise, Pontaza took no part in the baptisms. When he noticed this he spoke to the man who stood beside him in the square where the baptisms took place. It happened to be Captain Cardona.

"Fray Pontaza believes they should understand first. He is working day and night to instruct them."

"But surely it is best that they be baptized as quickly as possible?"

Cardona looked at him. "They are not infants. If they understand, they will be better Christians."

With the help of the people of Quezaltenango, a small chapel and some houses were commenced on the plains of Zacaha between the city and the high mountain range over which the Spaniards had passed.

While this work was going on, ambassadors arrived from the Quiché capital. They brought valuable presents and a message. The kings, Oxib-Queh and Beleheb-Tzi, repented of making war against their Spanish friends. They asked Tonatiuh to visit them at Utatlán. They were eager to swear allegiance to the Spanish king and learn of the Christian gods.

Alvarado accepted the invitation and prepared to move out. Quezaltenango had been pacified but there was not much wealth to be gained there. The gold and jewels brought by the ambassadors promised better things at Utatlán.

The morning before they set out, Luis visited the chapel

and cluster of houses going up on the plains. Fray Pontaza had insisted.

"I want you to see it, my son. I want you to see that conquest need not be of bodies and material things."

Though the friar still made Luis uncomfortable, his dislike had turned into respect, so he went. As he approached the little settlement he saw that the houses were all built like those of the poorest Indians; one-room affairs of wattle with steep thatched roofs. There was no palisade around them nor protection of any sort. Anyone could enter the colony unnoticed as he did himself a minute or so later.

On the roof of the mission chapel Spanish soldiers, nearly as naked as the savages, were helping them raise a cross. There was good-natured argument going on between the whites and the Indians, though it was obvious none understood the other's language.

"This way, Father?" one of the soldiers asked, trying to pull the cross to the left while an Indian tried to pull it to the right.

"Wait, my sons, I shall come up and help you myself." Hiking up his habit, the friar climbed onto the roof with the workers.

The sight embarrassed Luis. It lacked dignity.

When Pontaza climbed down again, he turned to Luis with shining eyes.

"I am glad you came, my son. Is it not good for the heart to see God's children working happily together? Come inside. I want to show you where we have placed the painting of the Blessed Virgin. The interpreter tells me the Indians call her 'La Conquistadora' because of her conquest of souls."

When Luis left, it was with relief and a lift of spirits. He admired the courage of those who were remaining but not their familiar manner with the savages, as though they were truly equal. He began to walk faster. No, he did not belong with such people.

chapter

🔲🔲🔲🔲🔲🔲🔲🔲

14

THE PRESENTS SENT BY OXIB-QUEH AND BELEHEB-TZI WERE only a token of the riches waiting for the Spaniards at Utatlán, the ambassadors had said.

Marching toward the Quiché capital, the soldiers talked of little else. How much there would be; how it would be divided; what each man would do with his part of the treasure.

Reason told Luis that his share would be small but imagination refused to be chained to reason. Already he knew how he'd use it.

As he and Bartolomé set out from Quezaltenango, each boy leading a horse and the foal running at the heels of her mother, Luis spoke of his plans.

"Some of the gold I'll give to the saddler to make a little deer-hide halter and lead strap for Preciosa," he said.

Bartolomé nodded. "That will be good."

"If one of those small gold ducks, such as the ambassadors brought, falls to my share, I'll give it to Doña

Luisa for her baby, when it is born."

"That too will be good."

"And one piece of jewelry I'll save to give my mother when I return to Spain."

"You return, *amigo?*" Bartolomé sounded distressed.

"Sometime," Luis answered. For several weeks he hadn't given his mother more than a passing thought, but ever since he'd heard of the treasure waiting at Utatlán, he'd thought of her constantly. Always he seemed to see her standing before her mirror, turning this way and that, admiring the collar of precious stones that encircled her throat. She would be pleased with a gift of such value, Luis knew, and boast about him to Tio Rodrigo. His uncle would have to agree that the necklace was beautiful, though he'd be loath to admit anything good about the giver. Luis' lips curled in a satisfied smile.

Luis had still one other plan but of this he didn't speak. It concerned Demonio.

"Some day I may find it possible to give him back," Alvarado had said the morning after the battle of Quezaltenango. Well, if this happened, money would be needed for his shoeing and a proper saddle and bridle. But Luis didn't actually believe it would happen, any more than he had at the time.

His eyes found Alvarado, a long way off at the head of the column. He was riding Demonio, and with a pang of jealousy Luis saw how smoothly the horse was going for him. No, it wouldn't happen, not even if Echeverria should die and the question of horseshoes be resolved. No man who knew how to control Demonio would ever give him up. Least of all the Captain. It was better to put such a hope out of mind and not speak of it.

From midmorning on, the second day of the journey from Quezaltenango, Utatlán was always in sight. At first it seemed only a hill with a pyramid-shaped peak and a square tower-like crag jutting up from its crest. Then as the army drew near, Luis saw that both peak and crag were fortresses built of great hewn rocks in varied colors. He pointed this out to Bartolomé.

"*Amigo*, look. How beautiful! Like giant mosaics. Truly this must be a city of greater wealth than Mexico in the time of Montezuma."

Bartolomé studied the buildings that excited Luis' admiration. "It is well that the inhabitants wait for us in friendship," he observed practically. "Otherwise it would be hard to enter a place so strongly fortified."

This proved to be an understatement. Surrounded on all sides by a deep ravine, there were only two entrances to Utatlán. One was by means of steps cut into an almost perpendicular cliff at the top of which was the pyramid-shaped fortress, and the other was over a narrow causeway spanned in one place by a wooden bridge twelve paces long. This was guarded by the square tower. For the army, only the second entrance was possible.

Up to the time she set foot on the causeway, Preciosa had presented no problem. For the most part she had trotted beside or behind her mother, and if she strayed a little, Mamacita's worried snicker always brought her back. Now it was different. A misstep after a playful buck and she might tumble into the ravine. A dozen times Luis' heart leapt into his throat as the little filly cavorted too near the edge. Finally, unable to bear the worry any longer, he asked Bartolomé to lead Alvarado's chestnut as well as Mamacita and he looped his belt around Preciosa's neck as a leash. She didn't take kindly to restraint and let out with her heels in all directions.

Luis was ordered to fall to the rear, and his protests that the filly would be even more unruly separated from her mother failed to change the order. So, encircling her four spindly little legs with his arms, he held her tight and let all those behind go by. The last to pass were two musketeers assigned to the rear guard, Flores and Oriza.

Contrary to his expectations, Preciosa acted in a docile manner when she was first released from Luis' arms. But this only lasted until they reached the bridge. There, the sudden upward flight of a small brown bird from the bottom of the ravine threw her into a panic. She leapt into the air and, whirling around, her hind feet knocked the musket from Flores' shoulder.

In helpless dismay Luis watched it spin through the air and fall. Both soldiers rushed to the edge of the bridge and threw themselves flat on the boards, peering over.

"The strap is caught—I think I can reach—" The words came indistinctly from below the level of the bridge as Flores' head and shoulders disappeared. "Oriza," he called, and the second soldier joined him in his awkward position.

"Preciosa, you miserable young one, pray to St. Francis that he may reach it," Luis scolded. "None but he would hear such a wicked little filly as you."

Then came an oath so violent that it could only mean
that the musket had slipped from whatever projection
had been holding it. Luis was so certain of this that he
started babbling while the men squirmed back from the
edge of the bridge.

"I shall pay for the musket, Señor Flores. Out of my
share of the treasure, I shall pay. The filly is young and
knew no better. But that is no excuse. I should have
controlled her. I beg that—" He stopped in surprise.
Flores was on his feet now. He had the musket. It hadn't
fallen into the bottom of the ravine.

"Alvarado must be told." Flores looked excited and he
spoke in a sharp tone to Oriza without even glancing at
Luis. The two soldiers rammed through the line ahead
and Luis lost sight of them.

What must Alvarado be told in such haste? Not about
Preciosa, because she'd done no harm after all. What
was it then? Luis pulled the filly forward and asked one
of the soldiers who had been pushed aside.

"Something about the supports of the bridge," the man
said. "I didn't get more. Flores and Oriza were in too
great a hurry."

"Please, señor, please hold the foal for me just one
minute." Luis put the end of the belt into the man's unwilling hand and ran back. He wriggled out on his belly
to the edge of the bridge and looked over. His head
swam with dizziness, but he saw what Flores had seen
and his stomach turned cold. The supports. They had
been chopped half through, and recently. Where the
chips had been knocked out, the wood was light and

clean. A few more strokes and the bridge would fall.

Far down in the ravine dusky figures moved. Still on his belly, Luis drew back. God grant he hadn't been seen, or Flores and Oriza either. There must be no alarm or the trap might be sprung at once. Otherwise the Quichés would be more likely to wait for night to destroy the bridge while the Spaniards slept as their guests. Even a boy knew that much.

By now, Flores would have reached Alvarado. He would have told him of the trap. Only Alvarado could decide what must be done. From now on the safety of all lay in his hands. That Alvarado had more skill and boldness than any other captain in all the New World was a thought to hold to, but it didn't keep Luis' heart from pounding and his legs from feeling like jelly.

When Luis entered the city a few minutes later, leading Preciosa, he could only wish it had been deserted, as they'd found Quezaltenango. But no, it was crowded with people. The narrow streets were jammed and the stone mansions around the central square were buzzing with activity like hives of bees. Servants ran in and out bearing trays of fruit which they passed to the Spaniards and the allies also. Everywhere there was a great show of friendliness, and if Luis hadn't seen the weakened supports of the bridge he would have been as impressed by the warmth of the welcome as were the other soldiers. He, too, would have been thinking of the rich presents, soon to be given.

Even Alvarado, surrounded by a group of nobles before the gates of a great palace, was smiling in a most jovial way. Dismounted but with Demonio's reins still over one arm, he stood in a position of ease as though without care.

Had Flores been unable to reach his ear? Did Alvarado, after all, not know of their danger? Did he not notice that among the milling crowd of Quichés there was not one woman? Not one child?

The sun was in the west and it hid behind the temple. Luis shivered. Too soon it would be night.

One of the nobles pointed repeatedly toward the palace as he spoke. Luis was too far away to hear the words of the interpreter, but it was not hard to guess that Alvarado was being invited inside to be received by Oxib-Queh and Beleheb-Tzi. Would he go? And if he did, would he ever come out again? Puertocarrero joined the group. Alvarado put his arm around him. Puertocarrero bowed to the nobles, they bowed to him, and there were more gestures toward the palace. Puertocarrero withdrew. Alvarado's smile became even more brilliant. He seemed about to enter the palace. Then at the gates he paused. There was another conversation.

Luis looked around for Flores. If he could see his face perhaps it would tell if Alvarado had been warned. But did it really matter? Any show of boldness would close the trap. No amount of skill could save them.

Bartolomé came zigzagging through the crowd. His eyes found Luis and he came straight to him.

"Go to Demonio," he said, breathing hard. "Make him bow to Tonatiuh and then snort."

"Bartolomé, are you mad?" Luis exclaimed. "This is

no time for pranks."

"It is no prank, *amigo*, it is an order. First the bow and then the snort."

"But why, Bartolomé, why?"

"I do not know. The Captain Puertocarrero didn't say." Bartolomé took hold of Preciosa and pushed Luis forward.

So it was Puertocarrero's order. Whatever the reason it must be obeyed. Luis made his way to Demonio's side and tickled him under the right leg. Demonio stretched both forelegs out and brought his head down until it touched his knees.

"Ah, my friend, what have you to say?" Alvarado asked.

"Tonatiuh asks the horse what he wishes to say," the interpreter translated.

The nobles looked interested. "Can the noble animal talk?" they wanted to know.

"To those who can understand," Alvarado replied through the interpreter.

Luis felt dazed. What was this all about? But the rest of the order. That, too, must be obeyed. He brought Demonio up from the bow and touched him under the barrel. The horse gave a series of angry-sounding snorts.

Alvarado spread his hands out in an apologetic manner. "He says the horses do not wish to remain in the city any longer. They are accustomed to graze at this hour."

When this was translated all the Quiché nobles began to talk at once among themselves. Then one spoke to the interpreter. Grass would be brought in for the noble animals. In the meantime a banquet was prepared for the Spanish lords and the kings were waiting to receive them.

Alvarado shook his head regretfully. The horses had taken a fancy to the meadow outside the city. They were powerful and important beings and he dared not anger them. They must be escorted to the meadow as they demanded. When this was done, the Spaniards would return and enjoy the hospitality prepared for them.

Again there was a babble of Quiché tongues. No interpreter was needed to tell of their disapproval of this plan. But Alvarado gave them no chance to object.

With a bland smile he bowed to the nobles. "Until this evening then, gentlemen." He turned without hurry and walked out of the city without once looking back. The army followed him. Alvarado was the first to cross the bridge and he did it with no hesitation or change of expression. Luis held his breath but the bridge did not fall. Horses and men reached the meadow in safety.

chapter

🮑🮑🮑🮑🮑🮑🮑

15

AN EXCUSE FOR NOT RETURNING TO UTATLÁN THAT NIGHT, as had been promised, occurred soon after the army reached the plains. A Spanish soldier, going out to forage, was killed by a rock rolled down at him from a hill. This, Alvarado turned to his advantage. Immediately he sent a messenger with presents to the kings, assuring them he didn't hold them responsible for this misfortune but urging that the banquet be postponed until after the funeral had taken place next day. In the meantime, he asked, would Oxib-Queh and Beleheb-Tzi do him the honor of visiting the Spanish camp that evening?

They came. Unaware that their plot had been discovered, they were eager to show friendship so that the Spaniards would re-enter the trap prepared for them.

The sun had already set but light still lingered in the sky when the kings came down the causeway, borne in flower-decked litters by men of noble birth. Alvarado, on foot, with a few of his principal officers, advanced to greet them and conduct them into camp.

The soldiers had finished eating and they stood around watching as the two parties met. All were curious to see these kings of fabulous wealth. Luis, in his place among the horses, laid an arm across Demonio's withers.

"Be proud, *amigo*," he said, "except for you we might not be standing here in safety. Look well at the men who planned so wickedly to kill us all."

Demonio swung his head around and nibbled at Luis' shoulder.

The little procession came on. Alvarado led it past the grazing horses so the kings could admire them. Cautioning the interpreter not to translate, he asked Luis to make Demonio bow to his guests. When the horse did so, apparently of his own incentive, the kings exclaimed with delight.

Luis was surprised to see how young they were. Their handsome bronze faces were as smooth as Bartolomé's and their eyes had no wrinkles in the corners. In spite of their youth, however, Oxib-Queh and Beleheb-Tzi were truly regal in appearance. On their heads they wore crowns of metal and jewels from which quetzal feathers sprouted like tropic foliage. In their noses and ears they wore gold rings and around their necks, gold collars of intricate design. White cloaks, heavily embroidered, hung from their shoulders.

After a minute or so, Alvarado led the procession forward again. Outside a shelter made of saplings which had been set up and decorated with Spanish finery for the occasion, he halted. To one side on a spit, some quail that had been shot on the march were roasting.

Alvarado pointed to them. His gesture was apologetic, as though for the meagerness of the fare. The kings' gestures were reassuring in reply. Then they descended from their litters and the whole party disappeared inside the shelter. And that was the last glimpse the army had of the kings for three nights and two days.

In the morning the nobles were released from imprisonment. They climbed up the causeway and then came down, followed by slaves bearing heavy burdens. Food in great platters of woven grass, and gold and jewels also, it was reported.

But the kings were not set free.

Again the nobles and heavily laden slaves came down from the city. Their offerings were accepted but the kings did not return with them. Among the soldiers bets were laid as to the amount of ransom Alvarado was demanding.

Several times each day Father Godinez or Father Diaz would enter the shelter. Once Luis saw Father Godinez after he came out. The priest's face was tired and discouraged.

Then, late in the afternoon of the second day, the notary accompanied Alvarado into the presence of the kings. Soon afterward Father Godinez was sent for. Word spread through the camp. Oxib-Queh and Beleheb-Tzi had signed a confession of their evil intentions. They wished to be baptized before they were executed the next morning.

"But it can't be true that they are to be executed," Luis insisted when he heard the news. "The Quichés have given ransom for them. They will be released as soon as they have received baptism."

He kept his eyes on the shelter, expecting every minute to see the kings leave it, but when Father Godinez came out he was alone.

In the morning the camp was astir long before sunrise. The soldiers stood in groups, talking and looking toward the shelter. Then when the first streaks of rose and pearl showed in the sky the kings were led out. Father Godinez walked beside one and Father Diaz beside the other. Their lips moved in prayer.

A few steps from two large poles which had been set in the ground and surrounded with dry twigs and boughs, a halt was made.

"Kneel, my sons," Father Godinez said, "and commend your souls to the Lord of Mercy."

Oxib-Queh and Beleheb-Tzi knelt and the priests laid hands on their heads. "May Almighty God have mercy on you, forgive you your sins, and bring you to everlasting life. Amen."

When the kings rose from their knees, they walked unflinchingly toward the poles.

"They planned to burn the houses in which we slept. They confessed to it," Luis said in a voice a little too loud as he watched.

"I know," Bartolomé replied.

"It is a just punishment that they burn instead." Luis shivered. The morning was still cold.

"It is just, assuredly," Bartolomé agreed.

Luis looked from the kings to Alvarado, who stood at

one side with his brothers Jorge and Gonzalo. He was laughing at something Gonzalo said.

"But it is not right—no, it is not—that Alvarado accepted ransom for their safety!" Luis fastened on this piece of double-dealing with relief to explain his lack of heart in the punishment of the wicked kings.

"The gold and jewels are no more than the ambassadors promised in the first place," Bartolomé argued.

"That makes no difference," Luis snapped at him. It eased him somehow to do this.

Bartolomé scuffed the ground with one foot. "It is how Tonatiuh looks on it," he said sulkily.

Luis turned his eyes back to the poles. The kings were bound against them but still they showed no fear.

Behind Luis and Bartolomé, Alonso Rojas was speaking to the friar Juan de Torres. Now that he was no longer talking himself, Luis could hear their conversation.

"Oxib-Queh and Beleheb-Tzi are men of courage. One has to grant them that," Rojas said.

"It is because they look forward to meeting our Lord in the glorious life hereafter," the friar replied.

"Perhaps," Rojas said dryly.

"But, my son, how can you doubt it?" The friar sounded deeply distressed.

"Your forgiveness, Father; of course it is as you say. But I have no liking for this sort of thing."

"You should have remained behind with Cardona and Pontaza, then," a third voice sneered. Luis felt the hairs on the back of his neck turn to wire. It was Echeverria who had spoken.

"No, I am a soldier, not a farmer," Rojas replied, and then to the friar, who was moving away he said, "*Vaya con Dios*, Padre."

"Now that he's gone, I'll tell you a joke." Echeverria sounded amused. "The kings do indeed look forward to meeting our Lord, but not for the reason the good friar supposes. They think it is our Lord who ordered them burned and that He must be mightier than Tohil to demand kings for sacrifice."

"I don't believe it!" Rojas exclaimed.

"Suit yourself. But it is what they told the interpreter after Father Godinez left them last night. The interpreter said furthermore—" The rest of Echeverria's sentence was lost in a long drawn out Ah-h-h-h! from many throats as a burning faggot was tossed into the tinder around the poles. The tinder ignited and licked at the feet of the kings.

"See how they dance," Echeverria chortled.

It was true their feet danced but their mouths made no outcry.

The heavier wood caught fire and flames leapt higher and higher until they enveloped and hid the kings. Then a nauseating smell crept into Luis' nostrils. Like the charred hide of an animal, but different. Perhaps it was only because he knew it was different that it sickened him. Luis stumbled away and vomited until the lining of his stomach ached. When he feared it, too, would be cast upon the ground, an arm came to support him.

"So your stomach is acting childishly again," Rojas said but his voice was sympathetic.

"*Señor*, it is horrible," Luis gasped. His stomach muscles were still heaving, though there was nothing more to come out.

"Yes, it is, *amigo*. To kill in battle is one thing; this is another."

A prolonged Ah-h-h-h! came from the direction of the fire. Rojas looked around. "It is over now. They feel no more."

Luis straightened. "Thank you, *señor*. My stomach behaves now. And after all, one must remember they planned to burn us. *Sí?*"

"And are we no better than they?" Rojas asked bitterly. "And do we make of our Blessed Lord another Tohil?" Then his voice changed.

"Forget it, young one. As I will." He turned and walked off. Luis saw him join a group of cavalrymen around a fire where breakfast was being made.

Luis went directly to the horses. He wasn't hungry.

The execution of their kings didn't frighten the Quichés of Utatlán into surrender, but the battles around Quezaltenango had taught them better than to meet Alvarado on the open plains where the horses were at an advantage. Alvarado, on his side, knew better than to try and storm the city. If he set foot on the causeway he knew the bridge would be destroyed, and the steps cut into the side of the cliff were all too well guarded by the tower at the top.

The conflict therefore became one of strategy. Alvarado tried to tempt the Quichés out into the open, and they tried to lure him into ambush. In this game they succeeded more often than he. Not only the ravines surrounding the city but all the nearby woods and gullies were full of hiding places and mazes of paths that led nowhere. Whenever the infantry pursued a party of fleeing Quichés, the savages would disappear and then reappear to attack from ambush when the Spaniards and allies were thoroughly lost. Most desperately Alvarado needed better knowledge of the country for this kind of warfare.

He tried to starve the Quichés into submission by setting fire to their crops outside the city. For days a dull haze hung over the plains, and the acrid smell of smoke. During this time the memory of that other terrible burning hardly ever left Luis alone.

"Forget it . . . as I will," Rojas had said, but in truth it was hard to forget.

The Quichés reacted to the loss of their crops as they had to the loss of their kings, with fierce anger but no thought of surrender.

"Their storehouses must be full or their bellies would be empty by now," a soldier told Luis when he wondered about this.

The war continued. Every morning the infantry would go out, bugles sounding, helmets shining, standards fluttering; most often led by Alvarado himself. Every evening it would return to camp no nearer victory than before. The horses now always remained at camp; they were useless in the narrow gullies and close-growing trees where the Quichés chose to fight.

The kings had been burned on the seventh of March.

In May the rains would begin, making travel hard. Before then there were many leagues to travel and many cities to pacify, but one day of stalemate followed another. Alvarado's temper grew short.

When the soldiers asked that the ransom treasure be divided, he flew into a tantrum. It would be divided when he got ready and no sooner, he shouted at them. Even with the officers he was testy. The roar of his voice was that of a bull as he strode around camp finding fault with everything.

"He has sent for the Cakchiquels to help us; they know the land," Bartolomé said. "When they come, Tonatiuh will be himself again."

"Why should they come?" Luis asked.

"They were once one people with the Quichés. Now they are enemies. Besides, two years ago, they sent to Cortés, swearing allegiance to Spain. Tonatiuh hopes their hearts haven't changed."

"Well, let us hope they come soon then," Luis sighed. "In the meantime I pity Doña Luisa for his disposition."

"You needn't fear for her," Bartolomé replied seriously. "Tonatiuh never beats her, no matter what his temper. He is impatient with her now because the baby, like the Cakchiquels, delays in coming. But he is always good to Tia Luisa."

As the month wore on and the Quichés still refused to surrender, Luis was glad to remember that one person, at least, was safe from Alvarado's sudden rages.

Every night in his prayers Luis thanked God that the cavalry did not go out and that Alvarado did not ride

Demonio while in such a choleric mood. Instead, Luis was ordered to exercise the horse within camp limits. Dismounting after one such ride, he was approached by Diego Sánchez.

"I need you to take a message to the Captain, *chico*," the blacksmith said. "Two of the relay animals have lost shoes and Echeverria won't give me iron for more until Alvarado pays what he owes on the last."

"Oh no, Señor Sánchez!" Luis begged. "Send someone else or go yourself. The Captain will explode with anger at such a message."

But in the end he had to go. There was a sick horse that Sánchez planned to bleed and the other men were suddenly busy also.

Luis walked slowly toward the part of camp where huts had been built for the officers. He tried to think of a way to word the message so it wouldn't bring a tempest of rage about his head.

"Excellency," he would begin, "most respectfully I beg leave to report—" But no. However it was said, it would anger the Captain.

At last, though his steps had become as slow as those of an aged tortoise, Luis reached Alvarado's headquarters. It was empty. Not even a guard was around. He turned away, feeling a great relief. He could go back and tell Sánchez that no one was there, and the smith could not berate him for lack of courage. But before he went, Luis decided, he'd stop and visit Doña Luisa. He hadn't seen her for several days.

The door of Doña Luisa's hut was closed. Luis

knocked and then, hearing her voice, thought it was to him that she spoke. He pushed the door open and suddenly found himself an unwilling part of an intimate family group.

Doña Luisa lay on a couch spread with bright cotton covers, looking up at Alvarado. He was holding something in his arms, beaming down at it with a proud fatuous expression. It let out a spunky little cry. The baby! It had come.

Luis turned to leave before he was noticed but Alvarado looked around.

"Ah, Luis, you are the first of my men to see our little daughter. Is she not a beauty for one not an hour old? Does she not already resemble her father?"

He beckoned Luis close and asked him to admire the small head covered with reddish down.

"She does indeed take after my lord, even as to temper." Doña Luisa gave a light, happy laugh.

Luis wanted to say something about the child that would please her mother but in truth the baby wasn't beautiful. She was red and wrinkled. Preciosa had been far prettier at birth. He stood tongue-tied and embarrassed but neither parent seemed to notice.

"This little one brings good fortune to the army." Alvarado jounced the child up and down. "No sooner was she born than a message came. The Cakchiquels are on their way, four thousand of them. Tomorrow they will be here. Tomorrow, with their help, we shall start to rout the Quichés."

With a thud of the heart, Luis remembered the reason for his coming.

"I, too, have a message, Excellency. It is from the smith. It is about horseshoes."

"Well, I don't want to hear it. Not now. Tell Sánchez so." But Alvarado spoke with high good humor. The days of waiting and frustrating inaction were over.

chapter

〰〰〰〰〰〰〰

16

DESPITE THE VALIANT HELP OF THE CAKCHIQUEL warriors, it took Alvarado longer than he'd expected to bring the Quichés to submission. There were days of bloody warfare when the sounds of battle, echoing from the hills, made the camp vibrate like a drumhead; there were other days when the fighting was miles away and could scarcely be heard. This was after the Quichés had fled the city. Wounded men and horses would come limping back to camp, and Luis worried continually about Demonio's safety. Then prisoners of war began coming in, driven in herds like cattle, to be penned up like cattle.

When the fighting ceased, though negotiations still went on, Alvarado ordered the prisoners branded as slaves with the big G on their cheeks. Baltasar de Mendoza, the Royal Treasurer, walked among them poking and prodding, selecting the youngest and strongest for the King's fifth share. The next choice went to the officers, and those that remained were divided among the foot soldiers who had been grumbling loudly because they'd received no gold.

For once Luis didn't regret receiving no treasure. He wouldn't have taken part of the Quiché ransom anyway. But when he was offered a slave, he accepted one gladly. The man had a skin wrinkled like a dried plum and no teeth at all, but Luis was proud as he led him off.

All morning he kept the man busy grooming the horses in his care, and in Bartolomé's, until their coats shone like mirrors in the sun. If the slave paused so much as to draw breath, Luis would make Demonio snort at him.

"Look, Bartolomé," he exclaimed in amusement. "See how he fears Demonio."

"I see," Bartolomé grunted. Then he said, "You will have to feed him. Have you thought of that? He cannot eat grass like the horses."

Luis hadn't thought of it. But Bartolomé was right. The slave would need food.

So far, except for the Negro slaves of Echeverria who ate whatever the overseer threw at them, there had been only a few traveling with the army and those belonged to the officers. None taken in battle had been distributed among the men before. Now there were many. Every Spaniard owned one at least.

Luis sought advice from a soldier. "*Señor*, I didn't think when I took a slave. On what are they to be fed? I have no money to buy food."

The soldier pointed to a gully near the causeway. "There is food there."

Leaving Bartolomé in charge, Luis set off. It was still early but he had no work to occupy his time.

"Bring some for my slave too," the soldier shouted after him.

"Gladly, *señor*," Luis called back.

As he approached the gully, the stench of overripe meat came toward him, but he had climbed down into the gully before he saw it. Breath rushed into his lungs in a gasp of revulsion. It wasn't the carcasses of animals but of men that lay there in piles, with graying bronze legs and arms protruding, and poison green flies swarming over them. So this was what the soldier meant by food for the slaves. Bodies of other Quichés. For a long moment waves of dizziness kept Luis from moving. Then he turned and ran from the terrible piles of meat.

"Why didn't you tell me?" he asked, returning empty-handed.

"I thought you knew," the soldier said.

At noon Luis took his own rations away from the cooking fire and shared them with the slave. There was not enough for two. That evening he shared again. By this time he felt quite hungry, but the infidel had to be fed.

The problem of food bothered Luis, and later another problem too. Dark had begun to fall and the slave sat with his back to Luis, staring up at the towers of Utatlán. When he spoke sharply to him the old man turned. For a moment his wrinkled face showed a deep unguarded sorrow.

He wishes he'd died in defense of the city, Luis

realized with a shock of understanding. As he, too, would prefer death to slavery.

The man was only an infidel, he tried to tell himself, but he kept remembering the look in his eyes.

Before he slept, Luis tied the slave's hands and feet together, but not too tightly. In the morning he was gone. Luis was relieved, although he pretended anger. He hadn't enjoyed owning a slave.

The last afternoon at the Utatlán camp, Luis was grooming Alvarado's big chestnut horse when word came that the Captain wished to see him. The horse no longer limped and Luis expected that Alvarado wanted to give some order concerning the animal. Perhaps that he should be saddled for the next day's march.

When Luis reached headquarters, a guard told him to go inside.

"His Excellency is finishing a report to the Captain-General Cortés," he said. "He will speak to you shortly."

Alvarado sat at a table, and on a stool at the other side sat the scribe, quill in hand. Between them lay enough sheets of paper to make a book. Except to acknowledge Luis' salute, the Captain paid him no attention.

"Read over again those passages I spoke of, Reguera," he instructed.

The scribe cleared his throat. "...I made an expedition and chased them and threw them out of the entire country...."

Alvarado smiled as though congratulating himself.

"... they sent me messengers to tell me that now they

wished to be good . . . I spared their lives and asked them to return to their houses."

"Change that to 'ordered' instead of 'asked.' "

The quill scratched and then the scribe resumed his reading. "I have liberated two sons of the kings whom I placed in their fathers' positions and I believe they will carry out faithfully all that tends to the service of His Majesty and the good of his lands."

Alvarado nodded. It had been a good decision.

Luis continued to hear the scribe's voice but no longer the words. His mind had gone back to the chestnut horse. If Alvarado rode the chestnut on the march tomorrow, that meant he could lead Demonio.

Alvarado had ridden Demonio daily of late. Sometimes there were parades to impress the new kings. Sometimes war games took the place of daily drill, to keep the cavalry from becoming bored or slack. Jealousy was sprouting in Luis like young green shoots of corn. Demonio went so well for Alvarado that at times he even felt miserably that the horse preferred the Captain to himself.

". . . Also be sure to inform His Majesty how we have served him with our persons and our properties at our own cost, for your own conscience' sake and so that His Majesty may grant us privileges. May Our Lord protect the magnificent person of Your Grace for as long as you desire. From this city of Utatlán, April 11th."

The words jerked Luis back to attention. The letter was finished.

But no, it wasn't. "Let us add another line," Alvarado said, and started dictating.

"As I am on a long journey and will lack horseshoes, if Your Grace could provide me with some it would be very well and His Majesty would be well served by it. They are now worth here 190 pesos a dozen and so we are trading for them and paying for them in gold. I kiss the hands of Your Grace."

The scribe wrote the words and passed the sheet to Alvarado who signed it with his large bold flourish. Then he beckoned Luis to come closer. "I suppose you know why I sent for you, Luis?"

"About the chestnut horse, Excellency."

"The chestnut?" Alvarado seemed surprised but let it go. "No, it is about the report. It leaves in the morning for Mexico."

The report! Mexico! So this was the reason he'd been sent for. He was to return to Mexico, too!

The sudden shock was so great that Luis couldn't speak. He should have expected this, but he hadn't. He'd been with the army so long that he'd almost forgotten how he'd come to join it. But Alvarado hadn't forgotten, Luis told himself bitterly. Not since Soconusco had there been an opportunity to send him back in safe company, but now there was. He was being sent back to Cortés from whom he'd run away.

Thoughts of Demonio, of Preciosa, and of the way Tio Rodrigo would smile when he heard of his disgrace, jumbled together in Luis' mind. All at once words were rushing out of his mouth.

"I won't go!" he shouted. "I won't go back to Mexico!"

Alvarado's face grew red. Then suddenly he laughed.

"I see you still prefer me to Cortés," he said.

He pushed paper and quill across the table and pointed to the stool the scribe had just vacated. "Sit down, my hotheaded young friend. I hadn't thought to send you back. Doña Luisa says it's too soon yet. Your ague would return in the lowlands and delay the messengers. But you must write the Captain-General. You must explain your action as best you can and ask His Grace for pardon."

Relief, though great, didn't make the letter easier to write, but with Alvarado's help, at last it was accomplished. At the end Luis wrote, "Should it be in Your Grace's heart to order it so, and should anyone return to the province of Estremadura, let my mother be informed of my safety." Below this he put, as Alvarado had, "I kiss the hands of Your Grace," and signed his name.

When this was done Luis got to his feet. "I thank Your Excellency for helping me find the right words," he said. "May I have permission to leave now? I had only half groomed the chestnut when you sent for me."

"The chestnut. You spoke of him before."

"It was about him I thought you wished to give me orders."

"Orders?"

"Diego Sánchez thinks the horse is ready to ride again. I have been exercising him daily and he no longer limps."

"Good. Have him ready for me in the morning then. I am pleased with the care you've given him." Alvarado did look pleased and Luis felt a warm glow of pride as he waited to be dismissed.

Alvarado didn't speak the words of dismissal. He continued to look at Luis while he fingered the long gold chain around his neck. Luis was becoming embarrassed by this silent scrutiny when Alvarado broke the silence.

"I had another thing in mind to say—one that Don Pedro Puertocarrero urged on me. But your childish outburst of temper has left me unsure of his wisdom."

"Forgive it, Excellency. My fear of being sent back was great, though that is no excuse. I beg you not to blame my lack of control on Don Pedro."

Again Alvarado fingered his chain and studied Luis. Then he asked abruptly, "Have you armor?"

"Cotton armor, Excellency, and a shield and spear I took from an Indian while riding in the battle of Zapotitlán." It was because of this battle that he'd lost Demonio, Luis was reminded unhappily.

"You'll need a steel helmet and cuirass at least. Among those belonging to our dead you can probably find some that fit."

But why, Luis wondered. Why steel armor for one who did not fight? Though he didn't ask the question aloud, Alvarado answered it.

"We have lost three horsemen here. Puertocarrero asks that I allow you to ride with his men when we go into battle again."

"Excellency!" Luis choked. He couldn't say more but his ears rang with the sounds of bugles and galloping hoofs.

"It will be a trial only," Alvarado warned, "so don't let it go to your head. And until then you will continue in your usual position."

"Yes, Excellency. It is understood, Excellency." Then he stammered, "Is it—will it be Demonio that I ride?"

Alvarado threw back his head and roared with amusement. "*Por Dios*, you would unhorse me, boy! Will you lead the army as well?"

Luis looked at the ground in humiliation. He hadn't meant the words that way.

Then Alvarado spoke more kindly. "You will ride a relay animal, one belonging to the expedition. Rojas will help you choose it. You are to ride beside him and take his instructions."

Luis raised his head. "I shall try to conduct myself with sense as well as courage, Excellency," he said with dignity.

"See that you do," Alvarado replied, "and now you may be dismissed."

chapter
🪺🪺🪺🪺🪺🪺🪺🪺🪺
17

WHEN THE ARMY SET OUT THE NEXT MORNING FOR Iximché, the capital of the Cakchiquels, the men were in high good humor. The sun was bright, the air cool, and above all the soldiers were glad to be leaving a camp where rations had become scant due to their own burning of the Quiché croplands. At Iximché, plentiful food and luxurious quarters were waiting for them. Presents also. Hadn't their new friends, the Cakchiquel warriors, promised all this when they took affectionate leave the week before to return to their city?

Only Alvarado was wary of the Cakchiquels' sincerity. "Let us not forget the hospitality of Utatlán," he'd warned.

So vigilance and discipline were strictly enforced, but there was joking also. "Has fatherhood made our Captain timid?" a soldier asked, and while marching a song was composed elaborating on this idea.

Even Doña Luisa, jogging along on her mule with the tiny baby Leonor in a cradle sling on her back, smiled at the words.

"Tonatiuh has not turned from lion into lamb," she laughed, "but it's true he dotes on the infant."

Luis, leading Demonio, was walking beside the mule while Preciosa frisked about her mother's heels just ahead. He glanced at the foal and then at the baby. No, Leonor was not pretty like Preciosa but her looks were improving.

At noon the column halted to eat, and Luis joined some soldiers of the rear guard who had come forward to give the baggage and relay horses better protection. Their slaves were with them, squatting on the ground, packs of their masters' belongings still on their backs, attached to leather straps on their foreheads. Only a few soldiers offered food to them.

"When we get to Iximché, the Cakchiquels will feed them," one remarked, stuffing his own mouth with flat cakes of corn.

"As for my slave, I intend to trade him there," another soldier said. "Perhaps a chief will give me gold for him. If he does, God knows, it will be the first I've held in my hands on this entire journey."

Well, that was probably true, but no reason to let his slave go hungry, Luis thought indignantly.

"It's too bad the Cakchiquels are said to worship a less bloodthirsty god than Tohil," the man continued, "or I'd be sure to get a better price for the savage."

Luis looked at him, aghast. "You mean you'd sell your slave for human sacrifice?" he asked.

"Why not?" the soldier replied amiably. "He's an infidel and so only an animal."

"But I wouldn't sell an animal for such a purpose!" Luis protested hotly. In a swift momentary vision he saw Demonio and Preciosa sacrificed like the dog they'd come on in the mountain pass. The thought was horrible. Just because animals couldn't know about the Blessed Lord didn't mean it was right for them to suffer.

He looked from Demonio, grazing contentedly a few yards away, to the hungry slaves.

And was a savage any more to blame than a horse for being infidel when he'd had no chance to learn of God?

The question startled Luis. He'd never thought of this before. But the answer was clearly No. He was as certain of it as though he'd believed it all along.

He wanted to shout it out loud but the soldier spoke first.

"I was joking, young one. Human sacrifice is abominable. It is one of the requirements of His Majesty that the savages give it up. I wouldn't sell him for sacrifice."

This was only a small part of what Luis had intended saying but it stopped him. He felt the comparison between savage and horse, though plain to him, would not be understood by a foot soldier. He would only laugh.

Later, though, he spoke of his conviction to Doña Luisa. She did not laugh.

"What you say is true, niño," she said. "Those who have not been told of our Lord cannot believe in Him. He does not blame them for this nor should we. I tried to tell you so once and you wouldn't listen."

Fray Pontaza had tried to tell him also, Luis remembered, wishing it were possible now to tell the friar he agreed.

As he trudged on in the afternoon sunlight, Luis thought of Pontaza for a while and wondered how the colony was faring. Then he began to think of other things. His eyes roved over the relay horses traveling ahead, each with a Tlascalan or Mexican attendant. The sorrel with the white blaze looked strong and fast. It wouldn't be like riding Demonio, but yes, if Rojas agreed he would do for battle.

The next morning after Mass, Alvarado spoke to his men before they resumed the journey. He warned them again of the possibility of treachery.

"It is true the Cakchiquels profess allegiance to Spain, and it's true they sent us four thousand warriors to fight against the Quichés," he said, "but we must remember that, there, we served their ends even as they served ours. Now the Quichés are defeated, they may turn on us."

Toward noon, scouts reported seeing bands of heavily armed warriors in the hills. Then the soldiers, too, began to wonder if the Cakchiquels might be less friendly than they'd professed. When, later, they saw a procession the size of an army coming out from Iximché to meet them, there were no more jokes about the Captain's caution. The rear guard came closer and Jorge Alvarado sent a man forward to bring back news.

Pedro Alvarado advanced until Spaniards and Cakchiquels met. Then the column halted.

"It must be the kings, themselves, that Pedro speaks

to," Jorge said. "The litters are even more magnificent than those of Oxib-Queh and Beleheb-Tzi."

When the man he'd sent forward returned, those in the rear learned that Jorge was right. The Cakchiquel kings, Belehé-Quat and Cahí-Imox, had come in person at the head of a multitude.

They were confronted by Alvarado who asked boldly, "Why do you seek to do me harm, when I come to do you good?"

When the reason for this question was explained to the kings, they assured Alvarado that the bands of warriors the scouts had observed were not armed against him but against their enemy the Zutuhils, who had been making forays from Lake Atitlán.

"Look into the ravines, O Tonatiuh," they said, "and you will see the remains of the slain."

With expressions of regret for his suspicions, Alvarado dismounted and embraced both kings and presented them with silver jewelry. Then he gave orders for the army to follow him and the kings up the causeway into the city.

When all this was reported to Jorge, his face showed relief. "Well, we can stop worrying, *compañeros*," he said. "The Cakchiquels won't turn on us while they can use our help against another enemy." Then he laughed. "I hope Pedro doesn't tell them it was already our mission to conquer the Zutuhils. He can strike a better bargain if they don't know it."

Luis' heart gave a sudden leap, like that of a frog. So they would fight with the Cakchiquels against the

Zutuhils! The next battle might come sooner than he'd dared to hope.

Iximché, like Utatlán, stood on a high plateau surrounded by wooded ravines, but the plateau was higher and also larger. It stretched three miles in one direction and two in the other, and included fields and open land

as well as the city. The approach, again like Utatlán, lay over a narrow causeway. In spite of Jorge's assurances, some of the soldiers grumbled that Alvarado was leading them into another trap. But once inside the gates of obsidian stone that stood at the top of the causeway, their fears vanished.

The straight wide streets were lined with small near-naked children. As the cavalry rode through, eight abreast, they threw flowers in front of the horses' feet. Women peered out in curiosity from every doorway. The presence of women and children was a guarantee against hostility. Nor could they leave without the Spaniards' knowledge because the mansion assigned to Alvarado and his men was that closest to the gates.

The faces of the Cakchiquels were not eagle fierce like those of the Quichés but had a rounder, gentler look. And the warmth of their welcoming smiles was obviously genuine.

The warriors who had fought at Utatlán greeted the Tlascalans and Mexicans as long separated brothers and bore them off to their homes. The Spaniards could hardly move for the crowds jostling to get near them, offering them garlands of feathers and other gifts, and making friendly noises. Large circles formed around the priests. The cross and a painting of the Virgin that they carried seemed to fascinate the Indians. They came close, one at a time, to touch them in wonder.

As Luis fought a way for himself and Demonio through the streets to the fields beyond the city where the horses were to graze, he heard Father Godinez expostulating. Every time he paused, the Indians shouted in loud enthusiasm.

"I'll wager he has thirty converts by tonight," Luis said to Bartolomé, who was leading Mamacita while the foal ran beside her. "And not one of them understanding any more than Preciosa does about our Lord."

He laughed but Bartolomé was serious.

"It is not for you to make fun, Luis," he reproached. "Even for those who don't understand, baptism is good."

"Fray Pontaza believes . . ." Luis commenced and then left off. This was not the time for argument.

During the days that followed, Alvarado's men were treated royally in every way. Food was supplied in great abundance and women to prepare it. One day of lavish entertainment followed another. Luis enjoyed it all but he wished the kings and Alvarado would get down to the business of the Zutuhils. Even while watching the exciting ball games that took place in the high-walled court near the palace, his mind would wander to the Zutuhils; and when he took part in the daily cavalry drills, the desire to ride with these men in battle made his impatience hard to curb. He had learned the commands and maneuvers quickly and felt himself quite ready. A suspicion that the kings and Alvarado had decided not to fight, after all, began to grow in him. One morning after drill he spoke about this to Alonso Rojas.

"Alvarado has every intention of making war on the Zutuhils," Rojas told him, "but he plays a game with the kings. He pretends he must wait for a reply to the messages he sent the Zutuhils from here, but this isn't true. Envoys were also dispatched to them from Utatlán, carrying the requirements for peace. Those envoys were killed and Alvarado had word of it; he is not obliged to wait further before declaring war."

"Then why wait, *señor*?"

"Because it is profitable to delay. The kings are offering him better inducements to fight at their side all the time."

"But it isn't right to delay for such a reason!" Luis protested.

"No?" Rojas smiled. "Well, the Captain is a good man of business. And you needn't worry, Luis. We will ride against the Zutuhils soon enough."

While he waited, Alvarado returned the hospitality of the Cakchiquels by putting on some games of war for their entertainment. In a large field outside the city he sat erect on Demonio, sun beating down on him, turning his beard to gold. Then at his command, the Spanish foot soldiers in newly polished armor marched and wheeled, while the allies, feathered and painted most fearsomely, made mock charges against them with long spears. The horses galloped in formation. Drums beat, bugles sounded, and the four small cannon, loaded with powder only, boomed so loud they seemed to shake the air. To ride in these games made Luis almost explode with pride. And not once did he mistake a command.

It was after the games that he and Bartolomé met Prince Tzián. A group of the royal children had come with their teachers and an interpreter to watch, and they remained to make a closer acquaintance with the horses. The teachers tried to turn the visit into a lesson. How long did the noble animals live? they inquired. Was it true they ate only grass? Were they born as other animals or did they descend from the heavens full grown?

Luis pointed out Preciosa pulling at her mother's teats a short distance away and the children rushed off toward the foal. With screams of joy the smallest ones threw their arms around her and laughed when she kicked up her heels. One pretty little girl put a garland of feathers around her neck.

Then one of the older boys left the group and started back to where Luis and Bartolomé were still rubbing the sweat from the horses that had been used in the games. He was about fourteen, Luis decided, as he watched the boy approach. He liked the way he walked, with a springy step that covered ground as though his sandals didn't touch it.

The boy's lips curved upward in a smile and there was eagerness in his sparkling eyes as they fastened on Demonio.

To please him, Luis tickled Demonio under the right foreleg and the horse stretched out his legs and lowered his head in a deep bow. Once was not enough. The boy, enraptured by the performance, wanted the bow again and again, repeating a word that was plainly one of command. At length Demonio tired of the game and Luis looked around for the interpreter to explain this. But, after all, it wasn't necessary to summon the interpreter.

When a Mexican chieftain came up and spoke to Bartolomé, the young Cakchiquel's eyes lit with pleasure. He, too, knew the Mexican language. His father had insisted he learn it.

And so a means of communication between the boys was established. In Spanish, Luis said Demonio needed rest. In Mexican, Bartolomé repeated the information. The boy looked disappointed but told Bartolomé that assuredly he did not wish to exhaust the noble animal.

He then introduced himself. His name was Tzián, and if the gods so wished it, he would someday be one of the Cakchiquel kings. When in turn Bartolomé made introductions, *Tlascala* and *Castilla* were the only words Luis recognized but the prince looked deeply impressed.

Before he left, Tzián invited Luis and Bartolomé to dine with him the next day. For the occasion, Bartolomé wore a heavily embroidered breechclout and mantle and Rojas loaned Luis his doublet and hose.

Tzián lived with his brothers and boy cousins in an annex to the royal palace. Walking to it through the gardens, Luis was astonished by their formal beauty. "Look, Bartolomé," he exclaimed, "have you ever seen such elegance?" In beds around high musical fountains, flowers bloomed—immense white ones like lilies that smelled sweet, and yellow shaggy ones like the manes of lions, and pink ones like shrimps, as well as begonias and bougainvillea. Trees bearing scarlet flowers and others with bunches of lavender ones grew around a small lake in which fishes darted about. From the branches of the trees hung wicker cages of linnets that sang and lovebirds that cooed, and many other birds. There were quetzals in the trees also, but none in the cages.

"Do not admire so much," Bartolomé warned. "We are being observed. You must not act unused to palaces."

"But why not?" Luis was puzzled.

"Because I told Tzián that you are a great prince in

your country as we are in ours. I wouldn't like him to consider you of lesser importance."

Of lesser importance! To Indians! Luis felt a laugh rise in his throat but he choked it back. He didn't wish to hurt Bartolomé's feelings.

"You shouldn't have told him what isn't true," he said, but later when thirty different dishes were served them in the banquet hall, he tried for Bartolomé's sake to act as though such fare came his way every day.

There were a dozen young princes at the table. They all wanted to talk to the guests at the same time, and for a while the task of translation kept Tzián and Bartolomé too busy to eat. Finally Tzián clapped his hands.

"It is enough," he said imperiously. "Now only I, as eldest, will speak to our guests." Then between bites he took over the conversation.

"Tonatiuh has sent envoys to the Zutuhils, asking them to come and give allegiance to Spain and make peace with the Cakchiquels."

This, Luis already knew.

"If they do not obey, Tonatiuh has promised to make war with us against them."

So a promise had actually been given already! This, Luis found of greater interest.

"The kings will contribute much gold to the expedition."

How much, Luis wondered. Had the final amount been settled or was Alvarado still trying for more? With Tzián's friendly and trusting eyes on him, it was an uncomfortable thought.

"The Zutuhils are very wicked people. They carry off our women and children and make slaves of them. Some of our warriors of noble birth have been sacrificed to their gods."

"Tell him we shall put a stop to this," Luis said to Bartolomé.

Toward the end of the evening the prince expressed a desire. "Tzián says he would like to ride on the back of a horse, as you do," Bartolomé told Luis.

"Say I shall ask Tonatiuh's permission," Luis replied.

When approached, Alvarado gave Luis permission to teach the prince. And so the next morning Tzián presented himself for the promised ride. Luis mounted him on Mamacita and from the back of the sorrel led him quietly around the fields. By the end of the lesson, however, Tzián was tired of the mare's slow gaits.

On dismounting, he spoke to Bartolomé in emphatic tones.

"What does he say?" Luis asked.

"That tomorrow he will ride the sorrel while you ride Mamacita. And there will be no line between you. He will make the sorrel gallop as you did in the games, only faster. He will make him run as swiftly as the flight of an arrow."

"But no!" Luis cried in alarm. "Tell him he can't, Bartolomé. Tell him he needs more lessons first."

Bartolomé translated this with polite smiles and many gestures, but the prince took offense and stalked away.

Luis feared their friendship was at an end but in less than an hour Tzián came running back, all grievance forgotten in his great excitement.

"Word has just come!" he cried. "The Zutuhils have killed Tonatiuh's envoys. In two days we go against them. Is it not splendid news?"

While Bartolomé was putting this into Spanish, Tzián embraced Luis enthusiastically. Luis returned the embrace.

In two days! his heart shouted. *In two days I shall ride with the cavalry against the Zutuhils!*

chapter

◫◫◫◫◫◫◫◫

18

Luis shivered. it was partly from excitement but also from the cold. The sun was not yet up and a heavy white mist rose from the ravines, shutting out all that lay beyond and turning the plateau into an island. In the central square of the city, that part of the army which Alvarado would lead against the Zutuhils was drawn up. Not all were to go; only a hundred and fifty infantry and sixty cavalry, it had been decided, besides the Cakchiquels themselves. No baggage was being taken and no food except what the men could carry.

The selection of Puertocarrero's sixty horsemen, rather than those of Chávez, had resulted from a throw of dice, though Luis believed his prayers had something to do with it. He couldn't have borne to be left behind in this battle but it hadn't happened that way, *gracias a Dios*. Instead, with steel half-armor over his cotton corselet, he sat proudly astride the sorrel horse next to Rojas on his roan, waiting for the moment when they would move out. The infantry was on their right and the Cakchiquel warriors on their left, facing each other across the square, while Alvarado faced the cavalry. He was mounted on the chestnut and, leaning down from it, was listening earnestly to Father Godinez.

The waiting was hard for Luis. Earlier he'd scarcely heard a word of the Mass and now he ached for Alvarado to have done with the chaplain. It was time to go. Even the horses felt it was time to leave. The sorrel moved restlessly under him and near the front, just behind Puertocarrero, he could see the gray mare of Gonzalo Alvarado humping her back as though getting ready to kick.

Luis turned his eyes to the left. They traveled along the Cakchiquel lines until they found Tzián. The young prince was impatient too; it was easy to tell from the way he shifted his feet so they seemed already running. Luis was glad that Tzián would be along. Bartolomé was not coming and after the battle it would be good to have someone his own age to whom he could talk of the feats performed by the cavalry.

"Men of the army!" Alvarado's voice rang out. Luis' eyes came forward instantly and he straightened in the saddle.

Alvarado spoke at shorter length than usual. It would be a forced march of seven leagues, he said, to the south shore of Lake Atitlán where the Zutuhils lived. Some of the Cakchiquels had already left the night before for their own villages on the north shore. There, they would secure three hundred canoes and more warriors and cross the water in time to join the attack against the enemy.

"Today, gentlemen," Alvarado raised his voice, "we fight, not for ourselves but for those true and loyal vassals of Spain, our dear friends the Cakchiquels who suffer greatly from the wickedness of the Zutuhils."

He paused to make sure there was time for an interpreter to translate this for the kings and chieftains. While he waited, a question was shouted at him.

"What about booty, Pedro?"

Luis looked to the right. Yes, it was Echeverria who had spoken. He was one of the two mounted officers in front of the infantry lines.

From Echeverria, Luis' eyes went back to Alvarado. Did he see him wink? It was too far to be sure.

Alvarado didn't reply to the question. When he saw the interpreter had finished, he again addressed the army.

"The Zutuhils have a fortress rock in the lake. When hard pressed they flee to it for protection and tear up the bridges behind them. Before the enemy learns we are coming, the rock must be in our hands. Until we are in sight of it we will travel together. Then the cavalry will advance at top speed and secure the bridges until those on foot and in canoes can arrive."

Here he spoke directly to the cavalry. "I myself will lead you, *caballeros*. I count on speed and surprise for victory. I also count on the courage of every one of you. It will be needed and I know it will not be lacking."

Luis' chest lifted and his heart hammered against his breastplate. This battle was to be a test of his fitness to remain in the cavalry. Pedro Alvarado would not find him lacking in courage, and with God's help he would not give way to impulse or mistake any of the commands in his excitement.

Bugles sounded the signal to move out. Alvarado rode toward the gates of the city. The cavalry fell in behind; then the infantry; then the Cakchiquel chiefs and warriors.

Those who were staying shouted and waved good-bye. One of Chávez' men called out to Rojas, "When you eat slim rations tonight, Alonso, think of us. We shall be feasting as usual."

Luis caught sight of Bartolomé. "Take good care of Preciosa and Demonio until I return," he shouted. He'd said this before, of course, but once more wouldn't hurt.

Near the outer gate that guarded the causeway, Doña Luisa held up the infant Leonor for Alvarado to see. As Luis passed her a moment later, she said, "*Vaya con Dios, niño.* May He bring you safely back."

Descending the causeway, the army was wrapped in cold, wet mist. But after they'd crossed over the ravine it was as though a curtain had been suddenly pulled aside. The sun shone and they could see into the distance where volcanos pushed their cones into a cloudless blue sky. At the foot of one of these, Luis knew, lay the Zutuhil capital, Tziquinahá.

The march was as swift as the country allowed. There was one sizable river to cross and wooded hills to climb. These caused slower going at times but the army met with no real difficulties. Nor did they meet with any wandering bands of Zutuhils. By midafternoon, still undiscovered, they reached a rocky height overlooking a level plain. Beyond the plain, water shimmered. Here

Alvarado halted his men.

He pointed out a long bay at the south end of the lake, in which rose a large island of rock with some houses on it. "It is the rock which is our first objective," he said. He shaded his eyes with one hand against the sun and looked farther north. "And those specks I see on the Cakchiquel side of the water should be the canoes coming to join us. It is time to go, and remember once we start our descent we will be in full view of any of the enemy who may be watching."

He took leave of the infantry. "Follow as closely as you can," he said. Then he turned his horse. "*Adelante, caballeros!*" he cried and plunged down the rocky slope.

Luis had never ridden so fast before over such dangerous ground. Stones slipped and slid under the sorrel's hoofs. Small avalanches of stones, dislodged by those behind, flew over his head or bounced off his helmet. Once the sorrel went to his knees but somehow Luis brought him to his feet again before he turned over. At first Luis' heart was more often in his throat than in his chest but soon he began to enjoy the wild ride. When they reached level ground he was fighting for breath but his eyes were shining.

"Well ridden, Luis," Rojas called and he flushed with pride.

Then the arrows came. A company of Zutuhil warriors, hastily assembled, appeared suddenly on the plain.

Alvarado attacked. Luis had no time to worry about mistaking the commands. The bugle blew and it was as if it shouted out the word, *Adelante*.

Abreast the horses galloped forward. Indians fell beneath their iron-shod hoofs, clawing at their bellies as they died. The obsidian-edged spears of the Zutuhils met Spanish steel, but the speed of the horses put force behind the Spaniards' thrusts that the Indians couldn't match. As they fought they screeched and howled defiance. The noise of it was deafening. Luis felt arrows and rocks from their stone-throwers strike his helmet but none struck the unguarded parts of his body. He didn't think of this happening; when he thought at all it was of those he killed.

"One less enemy for Tzián's people," he'd gloat. Or two less, or three less. When the tally was six he stopped counting but he didn't stop killing. There was no end to that.

The cavalry charged again and again, cutting through the Zutuhils' lines only to return in new attacks. Then all at once, the Zutuhils broke and ran for the fortress.

"After them!" Alvarado spurred forward. "Don't give them time to destroy the bridges!"

When they arrived at the causeway it was discovered that it was too narrow and the bridges too weak for the horses.

"Dismount. From here we fight on foot!" Alvarado bellowed. On foot the horsemen rushed after the Zutuhils onto the rock where the fighting was resumed. A few were left to guard the bridges.

Fighting from the top of a horse and fighting on foot were two different things Luis discovered in a rush that left no time for adjustment. It was a hand-to-hand struggle now in which the cavalry was outnumbered a hundred to one and all he could do was fend off one savage while a dozen others fell on him.

Where was the infantry with its muskets? Where were the Cakchiquel warriors and the reinforcements who were to come in canoes? Luis was down on the rocky ground with a spear at his throat when Rojas saved him. Then he was up and leaping at a savage who threatened Gonzalo Alvarado from the back. He hated Gonzalo, but now it didn't matter.

It was a desperate fight and almost lost when a cry reached them from the causeway.

"The infantry comes!"

Never was news more welcome.

From then on the battle was more evenly matched. Only occasionally could a musketeer discharge his gun without endangering Spanish lives, but when this happened it struck fear in the Zutuhils.

The Cakchiquel warriors followed the infantry onto the rock at a run. Luis caught a brief glimpse of Tzián. He was in the center of a milling crowd, smiling in a truly ferocious way as he laid about him with a broad-edged sword.

Later Luis saw Tzián again. He wasn't smiling. He was pushed against a wall and two Zutuhils were tying his arms to his sides and his legs together while others stood guard over the operation.

They want him alive. Luis' first feeling was of surprise. His next was one of horror. Tzián was the son of a king. The ring in his nose was the insignia of royalty. Of

course they weren't going to kill Tzián. Not now. They
wanted him for sacrifice!

He spoke desperately to the man beside him, not looking to see more than the steel armor.

"Quick, *señor*. We must rescue him!"

"And why?" Echeverria sneered. "There is more important work at hand." He turned away and launched himself into a fray around one of the Zutuhil chiefs.

Without waiting another second, Luis used his spear to vault over the heads of the men between him and Tzián and landed at his side. The surprise was to his advantage. He drew his sword and cut the throats of the two savages who were tying his friend before they could gather their wits. Then the others fell on him.

Tzián's bonds had not yet been securely fastened. He struggled out of them and reached for his own sword on the ground by his feet. Backs to the wall, the two boys fought a bloody battle. Luis felt a sharp slash above the knees. He fought on. There was pain but it didn't matter. He only wished the faces of his opponents didn't blur so.

Santiago! It sounded like a cry of victory but from a long way off.

There was another yell, near at hand. Tzián repeated it, shouting loudly. The faces in front of Luis were even more blurred now, but they seemed different. The head-dresses were different. Cakchiquel, yes, they must be Cakchiquel.

A whirling blackness rose up out of the ground. Luis fainted.

A NUMBER OF SPANIARDS HAD BEEN WOUNDED IN THE battle. They all lay together in one part of the maize field where the army was camped, across the water from the rock. Some were moaning or cursing in pain, but those less badly hurt were boasting about their feats of courage and the number of Zutuhils they'd killed.

Luis was sore and uncomfortable but he felt well pleased with himself. He'd killed as many Zutuhils as any man and he'd saved the life of Tzián. This he hadn't been sure of until, just before dark, Tzián came to visit him. Without an interpreter they weren't able to talk to each other but the prince made many sounds of affection. At parting, with a disparaging gesture, as though it were of little worth compared to the Spaniards' beads, he gave Luis an emerald from his headdress.

After Tzián left, Luis poked the jewel down between his leg and the bandage for safekeeping. Unless one counted the slave, it was the only object of value he'd received during the whole four months he'd followed Alvarado.

Night fell. The stars came out and campfires flickered. From the other end of the field came the sounds of singing and laughter.

"How are you, my son?" Luis looked up into the kindly face of Father Godinez.

"*Bueno*, Father, I was fortunate."

"God was with you. Have you thanked Him?"

"Assuredly, Father."

The priest moved on.

A short while later Alvarado came, stopping for a moment beside each man with a word or joke.

"Ha, Escobar, too bad you didn't see the end of the battle. The infidels were leaping into the water like turtles. Some escaped but most of them drowned.

"The canoes, Flores? They were held up by a wind crossing the lake against them. Otherwise none would have escaped.

"You want to know about booty, Arevalo? Well then, we sacked all the houses on the rock but we found nothing but a little food. May we have better fortune tomorrow when we capture the Zutuhil capital. And may you be well enough to come with us."

As Alvarado drew near him, Luis' heart began to pound. When it came his turn would he dare ask—? No, he knew he wouldn't.

Then the Captain was by his side. He put a hand on the blood-caked bandage above the knee and smiled.

"I hear you nearly lost a leg to the savages, Luis. It is well you didn't, for how could I promote a one-legged man to a regular place in the cavalry?"

There had been no need to ask after all. Luis sat up suddenly and pain shot through him as the bandage pulled at his wound. But the pain only added to the intenseness of his joy.

"Excellency!" he cried. "How can I ever thank you?"

"No need of thanks," Alvarado replied. "You earned the place for yourself today."

He talked about Luis' horsemanship, his conduct in battle, his aid to Gonzalo. Then he asked, "That vault you made with your spear to reach the young prince—was it because you remembered hearing of my famous leap on the Noche Triste?"

Was it? In the retreat that terrible night from Montezuma's island city, Alvarado, defending the rear, had been the last to escape. Unhorsed, with the causeway bridge ahead of him destroyed and the enemy howling around him, he'd used his lance as a vaulting pole to clear the water and gain safety. Often during the early days of the expedition, Luis' imagination had been kindled by stories of this spectacular feat. Lately he hadn't thought of it but perhaps it had remained at the back of his mind. Yes, it must have.

"It was in my mind," he said.

"I thought as much." Alvarado gave a nod of satisfaction.

After the Captain had gone on to another soldier, Luis wondered whether the leap had not been as much responsible for the promotion as his horsemanship or his skill with arms.

Toward morning, Luis' leg began to throb beneath

the soreness but he told himself it was nothing. It wouldn't keep him from riding against the Zutuhil capital.

When it was light, however, word came that all the wounded were to remain behind in the maize field. Bitterly disappointed, Luis lay on his blanket and listened to the sounds of the fit preparing for battle. First the drone of praying, then the clatter of armor.

At noon, the wounded heard that the capital had been found abandoned. They were to be moved there immediately to rejoin the rest of the army. The next day the Zutuhils would be rounded up from the hills. Luis felt cheered by this news; by then, surely, he would be allowed to ride.

But the next day his leg was badly swollen and small red streaks ran up from it into the groin. He was burning with fever and his head ached as though it were being crushed between two rocks. He no longer cared about the Zutuhils. They were not as real to him as the swarms of flies that clustered on his filthy bandage and buzzed around his face.

Afterward, he could never remember the trip back to Iximché, and only as something dreamed did he see the face of Doña Luisa as she soaked the bandage from his leg while a terrible stench came up from the wound.

There were long periods of blankness, broken now and then by the sight of other faces. One had a white beard, one a golden blond beard. They moved their lips but only gibberish came out.

Days passed. The bearded faces weren't around any

more. Then one morning Luis woke and his head was clear. He listened to a patter on the roof and knew it was rain. He recognized the flowers and fountains outside in the wet garden. In the next room a baby was crying and he recognized the voice that soothed it. He knew where he was. It was the apartment of Doña Luisa in the mansion the Cakchiquels had given over to the Spaniards.

A woman servant brought him something bitter to drink. He swallowed it and went back to sleep.

He woke again. It was still raining. He smelled pungent herbs. Doña Luisa was bathing his leg with a warm solution. When she saw his eyes open she laid a hand on his forehead and smiled. "The Blessed Virgin had you in her care," she said. "You will not lose your leg."

Lose his leg! Luis sat up, appalled by the thought. The savages hadn't cut it off; that he could lose it in any other way hadn't occurred to him. Then he relaxed. It wasn't going to happen. Doña Luisa had just said so. He would be riding soon again. He gave a great sigh of relief.

"The Captain promoted me to the cavalry. Did you know?"

"He told me."

"It is important not to miss the drills. I must get well quickly."

Doña Luisa pushed him gently back onto the blankets. "There is no haste, *niño*. There are no drills now. The cavalry has gone south with Tonatiuh against other enemies of the Cakchiquels. It will be a long journey. Tonatiuh also hopes to find the strait between the seas."

"But no! It isn't true!" Luis cried in anguish.

Doña Luisa began winding a clean bandage around his leg. She made no reply.

"Did Demonio go?"

"All the horses went except Mamacita and the foal. The Cakchiquels have built a shelter for them outside in the garden where I can oversee their care."

"And Bartolomé?"

"All of our people are gone except for you and me and the infant."

Luis swallowed. "Did you stay because of me?"

"No. Because of the little one. She had the flux. Now she is well but it is too late for us to join the army."

The rain had a dismal sound. Even when he and Doña Luisa spoke, Luis could hear it. It made him feel even more desolate.

"I'm sorry to have thought only of myself, Doña Luisa," he gulped. "Your disappointment is greater than mine." This, of course, he didn't really believe was possible.

She wound the last fold of bandage around his leg. "Disappointment is easier to bear when one is older. Rest now, but first I want to give back the jewel I found under the bandage when I first dressed your wound."

In front of his eyes she held the emerald Tzián had given him. It was attached now to a narrow chain so that it could be worn around the neck. Luis slipped the chain over his head. He had forgotten about the gift but he was glad it wasn't lost. And when he slept, he dreamed of his mother.

The next afternoon Tzián came to call. He, too, had

been left behind but took it with better grace.

"My father decided against my going," he said, speaking in Mexican to Doña Luisa. "I was disappointed, but Tonatiuh will lead us in many other wars. Besides, now it rains. It will rain for six months. It is a better time for school than fighting. Luis may come with me if he wishes. We would have great fun."

Luis scowled. Tzián was his friend. He'd risked his life for Tzián but right now his cheerfulness was too much. "Tell him No," he said to Doña Luisa. "Tell him I have no wish to go to school."

Tzián chattered on. Then Doña Luisa said, "Tzián will come here after school each day. He will teach you Cakchiquel and you will teach him Spanish."

Before Luis could decline this offer also, Tzián ran off. "The rain has stopped," Doña Luisa explained. "Soon it will start again and in the meantime he wants to play ball."

Afterward, Luis was grateful that he'd had no chance to refuse Tzián's second offer. Except when he and the prince were together there was too much time to brood. Envy and worry sat on his shoulders like twin vultures. He longed to be on the southern campaign himself, but since he wasn't, he worried about Demonio and Bartolomé.

Tzián loved all games and he made a game of learning. Circling around Luis' room, he would suddenly stop and point. If it was to the head, he could cry "*holom!*" and Luis "*cabeza!*" Each would try to be the first and often they both shouted out at once. Then Tzián would crumple up in laughter, but when he recovered they would repeat the word in turn until each knew it in the other's tongue.

When a thing couldn't be pointed at, Tzián would act it out, or if necessary explain what he meant in Mexican to Doña Luisa who would tell Luis in Spanish. By the time the infection in Luis' leg had cleared and Doña Luisa allowed him to walk about, he knew many words and phrases in the Cakchiquel language. Tzián knew even more in Spanish.

Luis' recovery was treated with great rejoicing by all the Cakchiquels. On the streets they hailed him in words which now he could understand. They called him "friend," or "great warrior," or "brother of Tzián," and when he gave them greetings in their own language they exclaimed with delight.

They invited him to the law court and showed him the sacred stone that told innocence or guilt. They took him to their temples and told him the names of their gods. Their chief god was called Chamalcán.

With Tzián and his younger brothers Luis often fed the fish and the birds in the palace gardens. He learned why the bird cages held linnets and even macaws but never quetzals.

"They die in captivity," Tzián explained. "Like the Cakchiquels, they can only live in freedom."

May turned into June, and June into July. In the corn fields young shoots had become stalks that were shoulder high. Everywhere grass was green instead of brown. Preciosa, grazing at her mother's side, grew large and strong, and Leonor smiled and gurgled at Luis as though she knew him.

Cut off from other Spaniards, Luis began to feel he had always lived in Iximché. He felt at home with the friendly Cakchiquels, whose love for all Spaniards was great. Hadn't the white lords forced the Zutuhils to make peace with them? And hadn't they promised protection forever so that never again would the Cakchiquels have to pay tribute to an enemy? Tzián's brothers and cousins became Luis' brothers and cousins also, and the rest of the world seemed further and further away each day.

"Say you will never leave," Tzián begged one morning when he and Luis were playing a game with small gold counters on a board marked into many spaces. "Are we not brothers since you saved my life? If you will stay, I will worship your gods. When your priests return with Tonatiuh, I will ask one to sprinkle me with water and give me a Christian name. I have thought of one already."

He threw out his chest proudly. "Don Pedro Luis Alvarado! Your name Luis, because you are my brother. Tonatiuh's name because he is the greatest man in all the world. Because I want to be exactly like him."

Luis looked at Tzián blankly, wondering what to do. He hadn't realized the prince felt like this about Alvarado. He didn't want him hurt. Would it be best to warn him now that Alvarado had faults as well as virtues, before his admiration increased still further?

Should he tell Tzián how Alvarado had accepted the Quiché ransom and burned their kings just the same? Should he tell him how Alvarado had tricked the Cakchiquel kings into giving him such a large amount of gold to fight against the Zutuhils when he'd intended to do so anyway? And should he tell Tzián that Alvarado would sacrifice his rights and those of any other person without a second thought?

"You do not say anything, Luis," Tzián complained. "Is it because you do not like the name I've chosen?" Then his forehead wrinkled in a worried frown. "Or is it that you think Tonatiuh will not allow me to use his name as part of mine?"

Luis smiled. "I am sure he will be most pleased." And he was sure. Alvarado loved flattery of any kind. But there was no need to say this to Tzián and he decided not to tell him the other things he'd been thinking either. Perhaps Tzián would never need to know anything but Alvarado's charm and good humor and courage.

"I, too, am pleased and honored that you have chosen 'Luis' as part of your name," he said.

Tzián's face showed relief and joy. "I am glad to hear you say these things," he cried. "Say now, also, that you will stay in Iximché forever."

Luis shook his head. "I can't promise that. If the Captain-General Cortés sends for me, I must return to Mexico."

Tzián sniffed haughtily. "Cortés? He could not make you go if Tonatiuh said No."

"He couldn't say No to Cortés. And someday I must return to Spain."

"Have you a brother there who is more to you than me?" Tzián asked jealously.

"No, a mother."

But by the middle of July, Luis knew he would never go back to Spain. Letters arrived from Mexico to await the return of the army. Doña Luisa gave two of them to Luis. The first was a curt note from Cortés' secretary. It said His Excellency had graciously consented not to charge Luis with his offense. Furthermore, believing him dead, Cortés had already replaced him in his household; Luis was therefore free to remain with the Captain-General Alvarado.

Luis' first feeling was one of vast relief. He'd expected more severity. Relief was followed by excitement and a sense of importance. *The Captain-General Alvarado!* So Alvarado had been promoted in rank and in all probability he, Luis, was the first to know of it. How proud Doña Luisa would be when he read her the words.

The second communication was short also. Luis read it and then read it again, refusing to believe what it said. It couldn't be true. But even as he assured himself of this he knew it was true. The cold feeling in his stomach told him so.

Tio Rodrigo and his mother had been married. His uncle intended making a clerk out of him in his counting house as soon as he returned. His conduct in leaving Cortés, of which Tio Rodrigo had been informed, showed he needed strict supervision and discipline, which his uncle would supply.

A clerk! It was a position as dry as dust. And with Tio Rodrigo? Never.

Luis read the note again, hoping to find, overlooked in the few lines, some message from his mother. There was none. There was nothing more except his uncle's signature.

chapter

🔲🔲🔲🔲🔲🔲🔲🔲

20

ALVARADO HAD LEFT IXIMCHÉ IN THE RAIN EARLY IN MAY. He returned in the rain late in July. From the highest spot on the plateau Luis and Tzián watched the army approach. It had been several hours since word of its coming had first reached Iximché and for over an hour they'd been able to see the lines moving across the plains. In the beginning it had been impossible to distinguish one line from another, or steel helmets from feathered headdresses, but now the soldiers, though only the size of grains of corn, stood out separately as men.

Luis peered into the drizzle. "Can you tell, Tzián, on what color horse Alvarado leads the column?"

Tzián put a hand above his eyes to keep the rain from dripping into them. "I cannot see the color, Luis." Then a few minutes later he said, "The horse is a reddish color but I do not think Tonatiuh rides at the head of the column."

"You are right," Luis agreed. "The leader sits in a lopsided manner, not straight like Alvarado."

But it was Alvarado, as the boys saw when the column started ascending the causeway, and they dashed down to the gates to join the crowd gathered there in noisy excitement.

The army was tattered and caked with mud. As it filed through the outer, and then through the inner gates to the city, the only brightness Luis saw was the flash of Alvarado's smile and that seemed forced. Tzián turned and ran beside the head of the column as it entered the great square, but Luis waited until the rear, too, came up the causeway.

Was it really Bartolomé he saw there by the baggage, leading a horse that was undoubtedly black? Yes! Yes, it was! *Gracias a Dios*, Demonio and Bartolomé were both safely back. The moment they were through the outer gates he ran up to them, putting an arm around each.

"Oh, *amigos*, how glad I am to see you!" he cried. "It seems a whole lifetime since you left."

Then something about Demonio's gait drew his attention. Not lameness, but a carefulness with which he set down his right hind foot. Luis bent over to look more closely. There was a swelling above the hock.

"Do not be alarmed, Luis. It is nothing," Bartolomé assured him. "Señor Sánchez says it will pass with rubbing and with bathing in cold running water."

"Well, then he will recover soon, for I shall take good care of him," Luis said, vastly relieved. "Did Alvarado use him kindly?"

"Always. But tell me about your own leg, *amigo*. How

is that? I worried about you greatly while we were gone."

With Luis' arm around Demonio's neck and his face laid close against Demonio's cheek, the two boys reached the square where the main part of the army was already drawn up. Alvarado listened graciously to the speeches of welcome and then cut the rejoicing short.

"We return as conquerors, *señores*," he said to the kings and people of Iximché, "but we have slept in the mud for many nights. We are tired and in need of rest. Tomorrow I will have many wonderful things to tell you."

Before then, however, Luis had an account of the campaign from Bartolomé and, as told by him, it did not sound so wonderful.

No converts had been made and, except in the first town, no loyal vassals gained for Spain. From most of the other towns the inhabitants had fled, taking their valuables with them. In one place a large part of the baggage had been stolen.

"The savages took all the clothing except what the soldiers wore. They took the extra strings for the bows and the iron also."

"Captain Echeverria's iron?" Luis laughed. This was a pleasing thought.

"Of course. It was all we had left."

Luis sobered abruptly. "Then what about horseshoes?"

"Until the Captain-General Cortés sends us some, the horses can go no farther. Eleven were killed. We took the shoes from them and with luck those saw us back."

Alvarado had been wounded in a fierce battle on the

coast of the South Sea.

"An arrow went through his leg and into the saddle. That leg is now shorter than the other. You saw how he rode?"

Luis nodded.

"In the next battle he could not ride at all, but watched from a hill. We made a great massacre; then all the people fled."

Bartolomé continued his account. It was for the greater part a tale of empty towns burned in revenge, one after another, until the army came to Cuscatlán. The people of Cuscatlán had sent messengers to Alvarado as he marched toward them, saying they promised allegiance to Spain and wished to be good.

"But while we were making camp, Luis, they fled, leaving their temples and storehouses bare." Bartolomé's voice rose in indignation. "They would not come back, though Tonatiuh sent, requiring them to do so, many times. So, when he saw they would not return he read a proclamation declaring them traitors to the king of Spain and sentencing them to death."

Luis was puzzled. "And if they were all gone, who heard this proclamation?"

"It was not necessary that they should hear it," Bartolomé said. "Only that the proclamation be read."

Luis frowned. There was something in this that seemed illogical.

"Afterward did he find any natives on whom to carry out the sentence?"

"No. We stayed seventeen days at Cuscatlán but the

people did not come in nor could we find them."

Had he been on the campaign himself, Luis wondered if he would have shared Bartolomé's disappointment. As it was, he felt a not entirely loyal sense of relief.

"Tonatiuh was in a fiercer rage than I have ever known him," Bartolomé concluded. "Not only because of this, and because he captured no gold, but also because he learned that the strait he hoped to find does not exist. He counted much on finding the strait to gain favor with the King."

The next morning when Alvarado appeared before the people, dressed and jeweled even more splendidly than usual as befitted one raised to the rank of Captain-General, the story he related was a very different one. A march of victory he called the campaign, where none had dared oppose him and where Spanish soldiers and Cakchiquel warriors alike had acted with conspicuous valor.

At the end he told the inhabitants of Iximché: "For your further protection, my dear brothers, I have decided to stay among you, building a Spanish capital on the plain beside your own."

There was much joyous shouting at this news, and at the founding of the capital four days later all the Cakchiquels flocked to the ceremonies.

Only a few hastily built wooden huts and a cross marked the site of the new city, but an air of such importance surrounded the event that the huts seemed as imposing as mansions. By great good fortune it did not rain. Sun shone down on the cross and on the newly polished armor of the army. It turned Alvarado's beard to its own bright color and gave extra brightness to the iridescent feathers in the chieftains' headdresses. Muskets fired volleys of salutes. Father Godinez celebrated Mass which Spaniards and many newly baptized Cakchiquels attended, and then the city was dedicated to Spain's patron saint. It was given the name of "Very Noble and Very Loyal City of St. James of the Knights of Guatemala."

Afterward, Luis, Bartolomé, and Tzián walked back to Iximché together.

"Muy Noble y Muy Leal Ciudad de Santiago de los Caballeros de Guatemala," Tzián spoke the words admiringly. "What a magnificent name that is; one to fit the beautiful city we will help Tonatiuh build. But more important, Luis, is that now I know you will always stay and be my brother." He gave a happy sigh. "We can hunt and fish every day as we've done this past month. And when you are ready to marry I will ask my father to give you my sister Icxiuh, Grass of the Moon. He will give you great honors as well."

"Do you forget you must return to Spain some day, Luis?" Bartolomé spoke sharply, resenting this new and close friendship that seemed at times to exclude him.

"I shall not return to Spain," Luis said. "There is no longer reason for my going and much reason for staying away."

Luis still felt some bitterness that his mother had married Tio Rodrigo, but the days had dulled his sense of loss. His uncle was rich. His uncle would give his mother the silks and laces and jewels that meant so much to her. As for himself, the marriage freed him to make his own life wherever he chose.

Luis looked down the horizon. Between him and the line of volcanos jutting into the sky was the wildest and most beautiful country imaginable. And beyond the volcanos was the South Sea. It was here, not in Spain, that he wanted to live. He wasn't yet ready to marry, no. But when it was time he'd like it to be a Cakchiquel girl. He'd like it to be one of Tzián's sisters.

Now that Tzián had settled Luis' future to his satisfaction, he turned to Bartolomé politely. "And you, Bartolomé? Will you always stay in the city of Santiago too?"

"I go wherever Tia Luisa goes."

"Well, since she goes where Tonatiuh goes, and he is staying, then so will you." Tzián laughed, vastly pleased with his own wit. "But now I am itching in this finery. Let us go and swim where the river is wide, beyond the ravine."

A week after the founding of the Spanish capital, Tzián was baptized. He had wanted this to happen immediately when the Spaniards first returned and Father Godinez baptized fifty all at once in the market place. But Luis had persuaded him to wait. Fray Pontaza had held that the Indians should be instructed first, and Luis believed this also. Sometimes he thought with amazement of how many of Fray Pontaza's convictions, which he'd considered foolish or fanatic, he had later come to believe in himself.

Father Godinez and Father Diaz gave what time they could spare to the young prince's religious education but, as they were busy seeing that the church in the new city was built correctly, much of what Tzián learned about Christianity came from Luis. While they fished in the river or in the swift mountain streams, Luis would tell about the Blessed Virgin and the infant Jesus or perhaps about the lamb that was lost. It was the miracles, however, which interested Tzián the most.

"Out of no more fish than we have caught today, Jesus fed the multitudes?" he asked in wonder one day when they were sheltering from a hard rain in a cave near the river.

When Luis assured him it was indeed so, he sighed with satisfaction. "What great magic, Luis. None of the Cakchiquel gods have been able to multiply fish in such a way."

"It was not magic," Luis explained patiently. "It was from God, the Father, that Jesus received this power."

"And the Father? Does He have power over thunder and lightning as well? Like Chamalcán?"

"He made them as He made everything else." Then Luis told Tzián about the creation. He listened as though spellbound and only once interrupted.

"In the first Cakchiquel man, corn was used instead of dust," he commented. "Corn is better, don't you think, Luis?"

By the time the baptism took place, Luis was convinced that Tzián understood about God and Christ and truly wished to worship them instead of heathen idols.

Alvarado, his most smiling and genial self, stood as Tzián's godfather and Doña Luisa as godmother. It was an occasion of much rejoicing, with a banquet given afterward at the palace of the kings. The happiness Luis felt in Tzián's conversion touched and colored all his thoughts. It was over a week before worry intruded.

One morning at sunrise he was bathing Demonio's leg in a stream when Tzián joined him.

"I have prayed to our most powerful Lord and also His Son and the Blessed Virgin to find more gold for us to give Tonatiuh," Tzián said. "They will hear me, won't they, Luis, even though I've only been a Christian for a week?"

"It makes no difference how long one has been a Christian." Luis stroked the horse's leg from the hock upward. The swelling seemed less and Luis was pleased. Then the rest of what Tzián had said repeated itself in his mind. It made him uneasy.

"But, Tzián, your people have already been most generous in gifts. Why do you wish them to give Alvarado more gold?"

"He asked for it," the prince replied. "But not for himself. He says the great king of Spain will be angry with him if he doesn't send more gold across the water. I should not like his king to be angry with my godfather."

Luis' hands tightened on the swelling and Demonio tried to pull away. Luis dropped his hands and sat back on his heels. There had been no complaint in Tzián's voice; only concern for Alvarado.

Luis looked up. For the first time he noticed that the gold rings Tzián wore in his nose and ears were gone.

"You gave Alvarado your rings?" he asked.

"Of course, and many other things. I wish I had more so his king would be pleased instead of angry."

Sudden and uncontrollable anger exploded in Luis. He should have warned Tzián, after all, of Alvarado's deceit and greed. He shouldn't have held back, hoping for the best. Well, there was no reason for holding back any longer!

"Let me tell you, Tzián," his voice rose shrilly. "It is only a fifth the King will get. That is his share. The rest Alvarado will keep unless he gives some to the officers."

"It is not the truth! Tonatiuh said all must be sent to Spain." Tzián was even more angry than Luis. "You are jealous because I love Tonatiuh more than you. That is why you lie."

He stalked off a few steps and then came back. "And in the future, Luis, you will please remember to call me by my Spanish name. I am no longer Tzián, but Don Pedro Luis Alvarado."

Later in the day, Luis found a chance to tell Alonso Rojas of his conversation with Tzián.

Rojas scowled. "Unless I'm wrong, this is just the beginning of Alvarado's demands from the Cakchiquels in the name of the King. He's not one to be satisfied with a few more ornaments. He'll leave them nothing."

"But they are our friends, and loyal vassals of Spain!"

"And so?"

"Surely the King will not allow it. He'll know how much is collected because of his fifth."

Rojas stared at him and then laughed mockingly. "In

battle you are a man, Luis, but in ways of the world, a child. The King will never know." He looked away with a shrug. "At that, Alvarado has something on his side. Cortés made him a Captain-General. He also promised to see that the King appointed him Governor of these new lands he's fought so hard to conquer."

"I don't understand."

"The latest rumor has it that the King intends to send over one of his favorites to govern here in Pedro's place. Pedro can't afford to wait to find out whether the rumor is true, or when the favorite is coming. Then it would be too late. No, Pedro must take what he can while he's able. There isn't much sense in leaving a fold of sheep for a strange wolf to eat or an orchard of cherries for another hand to pluck."

"But it's wrong!" Luis' mouth felt dry.

"Alvarado is no worse than the rest of us. Remember that, Luis. We are all alike."

"No! Not you!"

Rojas sighed. "Sometimes I feel uncomfortable. That is the only difference. And you, Luis? Don't you too dream of gold? Why else are you with us?"

The question shook Luis. Why? Admiration for Alvarado and a longing to follow him? Love of adventure? Yes, these had been reasons for his coming, but gold too.

"I came wanting gold," he said, "but it is no longer so."

"Well, it's a little late to change your mind." Rojas' voice was again mocking but he put a friendly hand on Luis' shoulder and kept it there a moment before he walked away.

Alvarado's next demand, ten days later, was for twelve hundred pesos in gold.

Despair was stamped on every Cakchiquel face. When Luis passed men who had formerly hailed him as friend, they averted their eyes.

Tzián came again to see him. "There is not that much gold in the entire country," he wept. "Tonatiuh refuses to lessen the amount and gives us only five days to collect it. If we do not, he threatens to burn or hang us. He says, 'Woe to you if you do not bring it. I know my own heart.' Those are Tonatiuh's words, Luis. Not the words of a king in Spain."

Luis knew Tzián's grief was not only for his people, but for an unbearable personal loss also. He ached in sympathy.

"We must pray that Alvarado will soften his demands," he said.

"I have, I have," wept Tzián. "But perhaps our Christian God is too far away from Iximché to hear."

"No, no. He is not! He is everywhere," Luis cried.

Tzián left, still weeping. For several days Luis didn't see him, so he sought him out in Iximché. Near the temple of Chamalcán he saw Tzián in a large crowd gathered around a Cakchiquel priest. Luis went back to the Spanish capital sick at heart.

On the morning of August twenty-sixth, the city of Iximché was silent, and no smoke rose from its chimneys. Not a Cakchiquel remained there.

chapter

🮇🮇🮇🮇🮇🮇🮇🮇🮇

21

FROM THE NEWLY FOUNDED CITY OF SANTIAGO CAME THE
cheerful sound of hammering. Luis could hear the strokes
of the mallets as he walked through the silent streets of
Iximché. It was three days now since the Cakchiquels
had left. Alvarado, who had sent out messengers promising forgiveness if they returned in ten days, still waited.
But Luis knew they wouldn't come.

Hoping that Tzián had left behind for him some token
of affection, Luis had visited the palace the day after their
flight. In the empty rooms of Tzián he'd found a message. It was laid on the board where they'd so often
played the game with gold counters. The counters were
gone. Stones held down the piece of cloth on which
Tzián had written. Because he'd learned so few of the
Spanish letters, the writing was mostly in pictures but
Luis understood it. It said that if in three suns Tzián had
not returned, Luis was to release the caged birds in the
palace gardens.

For two days Luis had come each morning to give

them water and food. Today he must let them out. As he entered the gardens a quetzal flew over his head and lit on the branch of a tree, its long green tail feathers hanging down in the form of a question mark. It eyed him with curiosity as he opened the cages one by one, releasing the other birds. "Quetzals die in captivity," Tzián had said. Luis ached with unhappiness as he thought of Tzián.

Some of the birds lingered on their perches. Luis left the doors open so they could fly out when they chose, and went back into the street. He wouldn't come to the palace again.

In the Spanish capital there was a great deal of noise and activity. Alvarado had moved his headquarters and established his government there the day of its founding, and by now there were enough buildings to take care of most of the needs of the new city, though more were still going up.

The church was almost completed. Father Godinez stood before it, giving directions to the Tlascalans who were setting a cross at its top. This was the second church Luis had seen built in the highlands of Guatemala. The other was the one in the colony at Zacaha, near Quezaltenango. On that one, Spaniards had worked too; on this one, only Indians.

Luis remembered that at the time it had embarrassed him to see Spaniards laboring like natives. He'd felt that it lessened not only their own dignity but that of Spain as well.

"Father."

Godinez turned and smiled at him.

"Father, have you heard from Fray Pontaza lately?"

"Yes, the messengers who brought the dispatches from Cortés stopped at Zacaha. The good friar sent me a letter."

"How was he? How was the colony doing?"

"Fray Pontaza was well. And the colony also . . . Careful there, my children." This last was addressed to the workmen on the roof.

"They are setting the cross wrong," he explained to Luis. "I must not take my mind off them any longer. The dedication is to be tomorrow."

Farther on in front of a hall that had been erected for the government, Luis saw a crowd was gathered. He stopped, wondering what was going on. Then he remembered. This was the first of two days on which those who wished to become citizens and landowners of Santiago could appear before the notary and have their names written down. Diego Diaz, the newly appointed town crier, had announced it several times but Luis hadn't paid much attention. He didn't want to own land; it was too much responsibility. Besides, with the Cakchiquels no longer neighbors and friends, he had no desire to live always in Santiago. He felt a restlessness.

Bartolomé came up and stood beside him.

"All the land being given out is not here on the plateau," he said. "Some is below. It is cropland and Indians are promised to work it."

"What Indians?" Luis asked.

"The Cakchiquels. When they return they will be assigned to the farms to work for the Spanish landowners."

"But that is slavery!" Luis cried out in anger. "And Alvarado promised forgiveness if they came back!" Then he relaxed. The Cakchiquels wouldn't come back. He knew it.

"Not slavery, Luis," Puertocarrero's voice corrected. With Echeverria and several others he had come out of the hall in time to hear this conversation. "It is the system of encomienda that is proposed. The Indians will not be slaves, but recommended to our protection. We shall teach them Spanish methods of farming and instruct them in the True Faith. In return they will work for us while learning."

"Bah!" Echeverria jeered. "That is just a pretense and you well know it. They will be slaves in all but name."

"You are wrong, *señor*," Puertocarrero rebuked him stiffly, "and I advise you not to treat those in your care as such. I, who am an alderman of this city, warn you."

He walked away and Echeverria spat on the ground.

"So much for hypocrisy," he said. "I, at least, am honest. I have no intention of coddling my Indians, or of farming them. I lost my iron in the south. I intend to get its worth back from the Cakchiquels in more precious metal. Some of the gold they brought in was from the streams. I shall set my Indians to washing the streams for more and I shall not feed them unless they bring it to me. That little popinjay princeling—Belehé-Quat's eldest—I shall take great pleasure in keeping him in the water until his feet freeze, if necessary."

"Tzián!" Luis exclaimed.

"Yes, I asked for him." Echeverria smiled cruelly.

"I would kill anyone who mistreated Tzián!" Luis was trembling all over.

The scar on Echeverria's cheek grew livid. He stepped close to Luis and raised his arm menacingly.

"What now?" Alvarado, himself, had come out of the hall. He was dressed elaborately. His face was complacent; his voice smooth, though authoritative.

Echeverria had no wish to tangle with the Captain-General. Since his iron had been lost, Alvarado no longer deferred to him. "Nothing, Pedro, except the boy was impudent," Echeverria replied, and went to join some others in the crowd.

He said if the Cakchiquels come back, they will be treated as slaves. Is that true, Excellency?" Luis was boiling with anger.

"Echeverria is a fool to say so," Alvarado growled. Then as though the sun had just come out, his face broke into a smile.

"And while we speak of Echeverria, Luis, I had been meaning to tell you. There is no longer any reason for me to keep Demonio. Sánchez has decided that though in time he may be ridden quietly, the horse will never be fit for battle again. Echeverria wouldn't want him, but if you do, he's yours."

The dream that someday Demonio might be returned had been so long with Luis that now he could hardly believe it was true. It didn't matter if he could never ride him again. Just his companionship would be enough. Luis' heart was warm with happiness and with love for Demonio, but the rush of gratitude he would have felt before

Alvarado started mistreating the Cakchiquels was lacking.

"Excellency, I do want Demonio. I thank you for returning him."

"Is that all you have to say?" Alvarado looked surprised and his voice was curt.

"I have wanted him so much that at times I have even prayed Captain Echeverria would die so this could happen," Luis said. "But about the Cakchiquels. If they come back, will they be treated as slaves?"

"*Por Dios*, boy, you are persistent. No, they will not. It is not permitted to make slaves of any natives except those taken in war. If the Cakchiquels come back freely, they will be our wards, not our slaves."

Luis accepted this statement but later he began to have doubts.

"Do you believe Alvarado about the encomiendas?" he asked Bartolomé. "Do you think he would see that the Cakchiquels were kindly treated if they came back?"

Bartolomé shrugged. "I no longer know what to believe of Tonatiuh. But this I do know. If the Cakchiquels do not come in at the end of the ten days he gave them, he will make war on them."

That night, although the horses were quite safe on the plateau, Luis went to sleep among them, putting a blanket on the ground between Demonio and Preciosa. He didn't want to hear the laughter of the soldiers or discussion of who had, and had not, already enrolled for land. He didn't even want Bartolomé's company. He only wanted his horses, and to think by himself.

Should he believe Puertocarrero and Alvarado about

the encomiendas? Or should he believe Echeverria? Or would the system work out, sometimes in one way and sometimes in another, with some Indians treated well and some abused? Of only one thing Luis was entirely sure. If Tzián came in, he would have no kindness or mercy from Echeverria.

Luis turned over on the blanket. He wondered if, after all, he'd interpreted Tzián's letter correctly. He'd taken it to mean that if the Cakchiquels hadn't returned at the end of three days, then they wouldn't come at all. But perhaps that was wrong. Perhaps it only meant they would delay in coming until firm promises were made, ones they thought they could trust. Tzián must not come in! Nor the others either.

Then, as though Bartolomé were with him after all, Luis seemed to hear him say again, "If the Cakchiquels don't come in at the end of the ten days, he will make war on them." When it came to Alvarado's plans, Bartolomé sometimes knew them even before the officers.

In war all Cakchiquels taken alive could be made slaves without question. It was the law. On Tzián's cheek would be branded the G, which meant taken in war. Luis couldn't bear to think of this indignity.

He rose and put his arms around Demonio. "What shall I do, *amigo?*" he asked. "Oh, what shall I do?"

When it was light and smoke rose from the chimneys, Luis went back to the city. He attended the dedication of the church, and prayed at times with different words from those of Father Godinez. He prayed for the Cakchiquels and that he might know the right thing to do.

Once, on rising from his knees, he looked out of a window opening. Crossing the gray sky was a flash of crimson and iridescent blue and green in swift free flight. A moment later something small drifted down past the window. After the Mass was over, Luis went around to the side of the church and picked it up. As he'd supposed, it was a quetzal feather. He looked at it thoughtfully and then put it in his pocket.

When a little later he heard a group of men talking about going out of the city to inspect tracts of land, he requested permission to join them.

Once he was off the causeway, Luis slipped away from the party and into the ravine. He followed it for a distance and then made for the wooded hills across the river.

chapter

᠍᠍᠍᠍᠍᠍᠍᠍

22

ALL MORNING LUIS VISITED IN TURN THE STREAMS WHERE
he and Tzián had fished and the caves where they had
sheltered from sudden thunderstorms. He looked for new
footprints in the soft wet earth, but he found none. He
listened, but he heard nothing but the drip of trees, the
scuttling sounds of small animals, and the cry of birds.
Some of the cries seemed not quite true, but Luis wasn't
sure of this. Toward afternoon he had a feeling that he
was being watched. He'd stop and turn quickly, but he
never saw so much as a branch or vine move without a
reason.

He dared not call out for fear a scout sent by Alvarado
might be in the forest also. At last he sat down on a
boulder and waited. There was a low rumble of thunder; a
storm was gathering.

He counted a minute out three times. Then a thick curtain of vines beside the path parted and Tzián stood in
front of him. Except for a breechclout in which he carried
a short dagger, he was naked. He made no gesture of greet-
ing; he looked almost a stranger.

"I am alone," Luis said, answering the wariness in Tzián's eyes.

"I know. I have followed you a long time to make sure. Why did you come?"

"Are you alone too?" Luis' eyes went to the tangle of vines behind Tzián. "Are the rest of your people far away? Out of these hills and ravines?" This is what he hoped; what he'd come to find out.

"I do not know where my people are." Tzián didn't meet his eyes and Luis knew he was lying.

"Trust me, Tzián. Am I not your brother?"

"You are not my brother, Luis. Our people are enemies. Tonatiuh called us brothers and now he seeks to destroy us. He talked of great benefits that would come to us as vassals of Spain. Now he thinks only of gold and ways of taking it from us. And of hanging and of burning."

"I am not your enemy, Tzián. I am truly your brother."

"No, Luis. All Spaniards are my enemies. You too. You have betrayed me once already."

"It isn't so, Tzián!" Luis protested. "How have I betrayed you?"

"You told me the Christian gods loved the Cakchiquels. Believing this, I left our own gods. I prayed to Jesus Christ instead, to soften Tonatiuh's heart. He laughed at me. He loves only the Spaniards."

"Oh, Tzián, don't believe that. Please. He loves all the world and everything that moves in it."

Tzián laughed scornfully. "Then why does he help the Spaniards to destroy us? Why does he pretend we are his children and at the same time allow our enemies to prey on us? I want no more of such gods. I have washed off the water your priests sprinkled on me."

Luis put his head down in his hands. What could he say to Tzián? How could he bring back his faith in Christ while those called Christians acted with such cruelty?

Tzián continued. "When the priest of Chamalcán spoke to us, I still hadn't returned to our own gods, though the others had. The priest said this, speaking for Chamalcán: 'I am the lightning. I will kill the Spaniards. By the fire they shall perish.' He said if we left Iximché on a certain night, this would happen before morning and we could all return. So all agreed and no one worried except me. I doubted Chamalcán's power and thought of the poor birds."

"You were right to doubt, Tzián. The lightning didn't strike." Luis felt a glimmer of hope as he pointed this out.

Tzián looked at him in bitter reproach. "It was because Chamalcán was angered by my doubt that he refused to strike. I know that now."

Luis didn't attempt to reason further. He knew it would be no use. He could only hope to break through Tzián's bitterness so he'd listen to his warning.

"I found your message, Tzián," he said, speaking slowly. "I let the birds out of their cages as you asked. As I did so I saw a quetzal and remembered what you told me."

"Yes?" There was no encouragement in Tzián's tone.

"That like the Cakchiquel, the quetzal can only live in freedom."

"And so?"

"Oh, Tzián, if the Cakchiquels return they will not live

in freedom. They will be bound over to work for the Spaniards. You will be given to the Captain Echeverria, the most cruel Spaniard of all."

"I know him." Tzián was listening now. "Well, we won't come back. We did not intend to anyway."

"But it isn't that simple, Tzián. If your people don't return within six days, Alvarado will make war on you. Your only hope is to go far away while there is still time."

Tzián studied Luis seriously and then nodded as though satisfied. "I am glad this is why you came, Luis. Now I won't have to kill you."

"Kill me! You intended to do that!" Luis gasped. He sprang to his feet.

"Oh yes. I would have had to. We believed Tonatiuh had sent you as a spy, or to deceive us with false words. But instead you came to warn us against him. You spoke truly when you said you were still my brother."

"Then you will leave, Tzián? Right away? You have only six days until he will come into the forest and hunt you out."

"We cannot leave, Luis. Though we live under the trees and vines, this is our home."

"But, Tzián, you must go," Luis urged in desperation. "If you don't you will all be killed or made slaves. Besides the guns, Alvarado can use the horses again. The shoes sent by Cortés have come. The horses will scatter and trample your people."

Tzián smiled. "No, Luis, the horses will not trample us. With your help we will destroy them first. Listen, Luis, this is what you must do. At a certain place we will prepare some pits covered over with grass and vines. In them we will place sharp, upright stakes tipped with poison. You will tell whoever leads the cavalry that you see us on the other side. They will all fall in. But not you, Luis. You will stay out and come and live with us."

Lead men like Puertocarrero and Rojas into a pit? Watch the horses impaled on poisoned stakes? Luis could only stare at Tzián. Did he really believe he would do such a thing?

The growl of thunder was coming nearer and great drops of rain began to fall.

"Well, Luis? It's a fine plan, don't you agree?"

"I can't do it, Tzián."

"But why not? It will be easy. I will send and tell you where the pits are after we have prepared them."

"It's not that. I can't lead my people into a trap."

"Your people, Luis?" Tzián's forehead wrinkled. "I don't understand you. You say you are my brother. If that is so, my enemies are your enemies and my people are your people."

"No, Tzián. Alvarado has acted with cruelty and injustice. But the Spaniards are still my people. Beyond warning you to leave, I will not betray them."

Like the lowering sky, Tzián's face darkened. "Perhaps I should kill you after all, Luis."

Luis looked into his eyes. Yes, he meant it.

"I am not armed, Tzián, but if you kill me I shall not blame you. You have great excuse."

"Well then, I won't kill you. Not now. But I shall do so in battle."

"I shan't be in any battle, Tzián. I shan't ride against

the Cakchiquels or any other Indians again. I couldn't do that either."

Before he spoke the words, Luis hadn't known he was going to say them. They had come from somewhere deep inside him without his planning. But he knew they were true. He would never kill another Indian.

Bewilderment took the place of anger in Tzián's eyes. "But how can you not fight on one side or the other? In this country there are Indians and Spaniards and they are enemies."

"It won't always be so, Tzián. There are some Spaniards already here, in a place near Quezaltenango, who are not enemies of the Indians. They think of friendship, not of gold. They are good men and more of the same kind will come."

"This I do not believe, Luis." Tzián's face had taken on a closed rejecting look. Luis knew there was no use in going on. Nor did he blame Tzián for not believing him.

"Believe then, at least, that I won't fight. Instead I will pray for your safety."

"To Jesus Christ? No, don't do that." Tzián spoke sharply. "It would only anger Chamalcán the more against me."

Rain was beating hard against them both. It ran down from Tzián's face and plastered Luis' shirt to his chest. He felt the jewel Tzián had given him pressing against his skin. He drew it up on its chain and held it out.

"We shan't see each other again, Tzián. If you will no longer call me brother, take it back."

Tzián looked at the jewel and the hardness went out of his eyes.

"No, keep it, Luis. I do not forget why I gave it. You saved my life then, and you have warned me now that the Cakchiquels are in danger. Our gods are not the same gods and our people are enemies, but we are still brothers."

"Thank you, Tzián." Luis' voice was uneven. "I wish the Spaniards and Cakchiquels could live together in peace. I wish we could always hunt and fish together, and our sons also. I would have liked things to turn out that way."

"I, too, Luis." Tzián's voice was sad. "I shall often think and wonder about you."

"And I will think of you."

"One thing I wonder about right now, Luis. If you don't fight at all, what will you do?"

Luis had no answer. "I don't know what I'll do, Tzián. I have only known for a few minutes what I won't do."

There came a great clap of thunder, and lightning zigzagged across the sky in the west.

Neither boy moved. Both knew that when they did, it would be to separate forever. And so they stood, with all that could be said between them, said.

At last Luis could bear it no longer. "I must leave. Soon it will be too dark to see the path. My eyes are not as keen as yours, Tzián."

They embraced, and drew apart.

Tzián climbed up the rocky hillside and Luis started back along the path to Santiago. He didn't look around. He knew Tzián wouldn't either.

Again thunder crashed and lightning flashed in the west. In that direction lay Quezaltenango and Zacaha.

chapter

23

THE STORM THAT HAD RAGED THROUGH THE NIGHT WAS over. The sun, a rare gift, was shining down on the city of Santiago. Soldiers were drilling in the field outside it, and the sound of a bugle and an occasional sharp command carried into army headquarters where Alvarado sat at his desk and Luis stood facing him.

"You want to leave my army? Now? When only recently I promoted you to the cavalry?" Alvarado looked astounded, as though such a thing couldn't be.

Luis straightened his shoulders. All night he'd lain awake, thinking of this interview. He was more than a little nervous.

"Yes, Excellency. I ask permission to take my horses and go."

"Is it to return to Cortés?" Alvarado's eyes narrowed a little as they always did when he spoke of Cortés. "Don't you know there is more gold and land here than he has ever won?"

"Excellency—"

"The Cakchiquels won't come in; I'm sure of it. Would you miss a chance to ride against them? It will be a greater battle than the one against the Zutuhils. Have you thought of that?"

"I've thought of it, Excellency." Luis' fingernails bit into his palms. "It's—"

"Don't interrupt, boy," Alvarado reprimanded impatiently, as though he hadn't asked a question. "I hear the Cakchiquels have gold hidden away in caves. And there is more in the streams. If you took up land here in Santiago you could have slaves to wash the streams for you. There is still time to enroll."

Luis opened his mouth and then shut it.

"When the rainy season is over, there are other great cities toward the North Sea, waiting to be conquered. I am told they are more full of riches than any cities we've seen yet."

Alvarado's eyes shone when he spoke of the riches and his voice rose as though he were addressing the army instead of one boy.

"As a member of the cavalry your share will be greater than before."

Greater? So far he had received nothing.

"I want no gold, Excellency." Luis knew he was risking another reprimand by speaking but he could listen no longer. "And furthermore, I relinquish all claim to what is owed me."

"*Por Dios*, Luis, are you crazy?" Alvarado's tone changed suddenly from the one he used to rouse the army to one of disbelief.

"No, Excellency, I am not crazy. It's just that I've had enough of killing Indians. I will do no more of it." There. It was said at last.

Alvarado looked down at his desk. His fingers drummed on it.

"So? You will kill no more Indians." His voice had become calm, ominously calm. "You seem to forget it is I who make the decisions."

"Not this one. I came to it by myself. I shall not fight against the Cakchiquels nor any other Indians again." Luis hoped that the desk hid his knees from Alvarado. They were trembling.

"And if I order it?"

"I shall refuse." Luis looked into Alvarado's eyes. Their bright blue seemed to have darkened, as the sky before a storm.

"Would you enjoy hanging, boy?" the voice rumbled.

A sweat broke out on Luis' forehead but his eyes never left Alvarado's.

"No, I should not, Excellency. I should not enjoy it at all. But I do not question your authority to order it."

Luis braced himself for the storm he knew was about to break. It came with a roar. Alvarado was making noises like an angry bull. The walls seemed to shake with it. Alvarado was shaking too. Then something seemed to change, although Alvarado continued to shake and roar. No, it couldn't be. Yes, it was. Alvarado was laughing.

"It's good of you to leave me some authority, Luis," he wheezed at last. "And to be honest, I should not enjoy your hanging either. You are a hotheaded young cockerel but I have a fondness for you. So has Doña Luisa."

"Then—"

"Wait. If the Cakchiquels don't come in—and I don't believe they will—I'd have to hang you if you refused to ride out and fight against them. Yes, you had better leave as you asked. But where will you go? What will you do?"

This time Luis knew. "I want to return to Zacaha and work at the mission with Fray Pontaza."

"Pontaza!" There was relief in Alvarado's voice. "Well, by all the saints, why didn't you say so? We need not have had all this talk of hanging."

"I tried at first, Excellency."

"But I should warn you, Luis. Hanging might be kinder after all. Pontaza is a dreamer. Indians can't be treated as equals. He will find that out when they rise against him. It is only a question of time until the colony is wiped out."

"You allowed him to found it as he pleased," Luis reminded him.

"Of course. He is a Franciscan, sent over by the King. Even for his own good I could not interfere with him."

"I have your permission, then, Excellency?"

Alvarado sighed. "Yes, Luis, go if you wish. It is a four days' journey, though. Without an escort I doubt if you'll reach there safely."

"I will, Excellency. I know I will."

"If you ask it, I'll let you have one Indian as company."

"Bartolomé?"

"Speak to Doña Luisa. He is her nephew. Well, Luis, go with God." Suddenly he smiled. "We have had our disagreements, but I shall miss you."

"*Gracias*, Excellency. And I shall miss you also." It was true. Alvarado was not a man it would be easy to forget.

In the house of Doña Luisa, the little Leonor waved her arms and legs about in a woven reed cradle that Bartolomé was keeping in motion. After Luis had told of his plans, he went over and put one finger into the baby's fist.

"Good-bye, little sister," he said. "I hope we will meet again."

Doña Luisa looked at him with worried eyes. "It is a long journey to Zacaha," she said. "Are you sure, Luis, that your heart lies there?"

"Quite sure, Doña Luisa. It is what I want to do above all things. And as for the journey, the Captain-General has given leave for Bartolomé to come with me if you agree."

"Then go, Bartolomé," she urged her nephew.

"No, Tia Luisa, my place is here with you. But, Luis, I shall pray for your safety. You will always be in my thoughts. How soon are you starting?"

"Right away, Bartolomé. As soon as I finish my fare-wells and gather my belongings together."

"I'll see to your provisions, then. You take the horses?"

"Yes, both."

"I shall be waiting in the pasture, *amigo*."

When he had gone, Doña Luisa sighed. "I, too, shall pray for your safety, Luis. You are as dear to me as a son."

"And you are more my mother than my real one." There was a blur in front of Luis' eyes as he left her.

It wasn't easy to say these last good-byes. To Diego Sánchez; to Alonso Rojas; to Captain Puertocarrero. And there was a tight knot in his chest when he made his last confession to Father Godinez.

Walking out of the church together afterward, Luis told him why he was leaving.

"At one time, Father, I didn't believe Fray Pontaza—that the Indians are people as we are, and to take their land and freedom is wrong. Now I do believe it. I have seen the Cakchiquels turn away from God because they were unjustly treated."

Father Godinez sighed. "I, too, believe it, but here all I can do is pray."

"It is why I must return to Zacaha. There I saw Spaniards and Indians working together as friends. I want to work with them."

Father Godinez looked at him closely. "Tell me, Luis, do you feel a calling? Would you like to study for the priesthood?"

"I don't know, Father. For now, I only want to help at the mission."

When all his farewells were finished, Luis made a bundle of his extra clothes and picked up the bow that Tzián had given him. A light one, for game not war.

In the pasture Bartolomé had Demonio and Preciosa ready, and food in a small pack strapped on Demonio's back.

"I will walk down the causeway with you, Luis," he said.

It was like so many other times when, each leading a horse, they had traveled together. Luis wished it could be so on this journey also, but Bartolomé held to his decision.

"You do not need me, Luis, and Tia Luisa does. The slaughter of the Cakchiquels is going to grieve her sorely.

She learned to love them as you did."

At the bottom of the causeway they parted.

"We will meet again, Bartolomé."

"I am sure of that, too, Luis."

As he walked west, the sun was above Luis' head, and

then in his eyes. At first it felt strange and lonely to be traveling without the column in front and behind, but the farther he went from Iximché and Santiago, the less Luis minded this. He was not afraid.

Late in the afternoon he made camp beside a stream. From his pack he took some flat cakes of corn. There were enough to last four days. He watched Demonio and Preciosa grazing in contentment nearby. It was good to have them to love and talk to.

"Do you know what I have in mind for you, my children?" he asked. "No? Then I shall tell you. In the colony there are no horses, but you shall see to that. When Preciosa is old enough, you shall have foals; one each year. In time your grandchildren will cover the plains of Zacaha."

The air was sweet and smelled of pine; the grass was dry enough to lie on with pleasure. Luis stretched out and looked up into the sky. Then his hand went into his pocket, touching his quetzal feather.

some notes on history

some notes on history

🔳🔳🔳🔳🔳🔳🔳🔳🔳🔳🔳🔳🔳🔳🔳🔳🔳🔳🔳🔳🔳🔳🔳🔳🔳

IT IS ALMOST CERTAIN THAT IN TIME THE INDIANS OF Guatemala would have been conquered by white men—indeed their own ancient beliefs foretold the coming of white lords—but the conquest was expedited by affairs in Europe.

In the late fifteenth century intelligent men already believed the world was a sphere but no one as yet had proved it by physical circumvention. Christopher Columbus had a burning desire to take the first step in this direction; to reach the Orient which lay to the east by sailing west. For this he needed backers to finance him and a reason for their doing so that would benefit them. The reason wasn't hard to find. At that time Italy held a monopoly on the rich trade with the Orient over the established route through the Mediterranean and the Levant. To share in this lucrative trade, the rest of Europe needed an alternate route.

Columbus tried first to interest Portugal, as it was the foremost center of navigation. However, Portuguese explorations along the coast of Africa led its king to believe the best route to the Far East lay around the tip of that continent.

In 1486, Columbus laid his plan before Ferdinand and Isabella. The Spanish sovereigns were interested but there were years of delay while they were expending all their energies and resources on a war to oust the Moors from Granada, the last Mohammedan stronghold in Christian Spain. At last, though, the Moors were vanquished in January of 1492, and in April of that year final agreements with Columbus were signed.

As all know, Columbus never found the western trade route to the Orient he promised Ferdinand and Isabella, but the islands on which he landed and established colonies soon proved valuable to Spain. At first everyone thought, as Columbus did, that they lay off the coast of India. Believing that permanent settlers would strengthen her claim to the "Indies," Spain offered colonists free land and in some cases free passage.

From the beginning the islands attracted restless young Spaniards released from warfare against the Moors. Love of adventure, hopes of getting rich, and missionary zeal were all motivating factors. The gold masks and nuggets brought back by Columbus from his first voyage whetted their imaginations, and the Indians he brought back were as plainly lacking in Christian faith as the Moors.

Among the men who crossed the Atlantic in the early 1500's were the two directly responsible for Guatemala's conquest. The first, coming in 1504, was Hernán Cortés. The other, coming in 1510 with numerous brothers and cousins, was Pedro de Alvarado. Both men started by cultivating their lands but neither enjoyed farming. When opportunity offered a more exciting way of life they seized on it eagerly.

After the settled islands became crowded, there was an expansion, first to the unpopulated islands and then to the mainland.

In 1517, the Governor of Cuba, Diego Velásquez, decided on mainland explorations of his own and backed three expeditions. All of these sailed in the direction of Yucatan. The second expedition, headed by Velásquez' nephew, Juan de Grijalva, rounded the Yucatan peninsula. At Tobasco, the Spaniards first heard of Mexico. This, they were told, was a country to the west fabulously rich in gold. Pedro Alvarado was on this expedition.

When the third expedition sailed from Cuba in 1519 with Cortés as its leader, Alvarado was again along. While at sea he captained one of the eleven ships, and on land was one of Cortés' foremost officers. Cortés followed the route of Grijalva to Vera Cruz. There he received rich gifts from the Mexican ruler, Montezuma, and the plea that he should not visit him. The gifts settled the fate of Mexico and thus of Guatemala.

From Vera Cruz, Cortés' army struck inland toward the heart of Mexico, Montezuma's capital, built on an island in the middle of a large lake. On the way the army passed through the independent kingdom of Tlascala, which was under continual harassment by Montezuma. These people offered Cortés fierce resistance, but when defeated they became Spain's staunchest allies in the New World. Without their help neither Mexico nor Guatemala might have fallen such certain victims. When on the famous Noche

Triste Cortés was forced to abandon the Mexican capital, it was the Tlascalans who gave the Spanish army aid and shelter in their own country. A year later they helped Cortés recapture the capital.

The treasure of the Aztec monarch Montezuma was the first great wealth the Spaniards found in the New World. Soon rumors of equal wealth among the Mayan Indians of Guatemala began to reach the ears of Cortés. On December sixth of 1523 he sent out a large expedition to conquer this vast and distant territory for Spain, putting at its head Pedro Alvarado.

Alvarado's instructions from Cortés, according to Bernal Díaz del Castillo, the renowned chronicler who accompanied the Mexican expedition, were highly humane. Alvarado was "to strive by every means to gain the inhabitants by kindness and friendship," and the clergy accompanying him were "to make every exertion to induce the inhabitants to abolish their human sacrifices and other abominations and to lead them into the bosom of our holy Christian Church." Díaz doesn't mention anything being said about gold but surely it must have been spoken of. As to the other instructions, history records in what measure they were obeyed.

In *The Quetzal Feather*, I have told what happened in Guatemala during the days of the Conquest up to the founding of the Spanish capital Santiago, and the flight of the Cakchiquels from their capital, Iximché. Later Guatemalan history must be found in other books, but to tie up some loose threads I feel the reader is owed a few further bits of information.

A fierce war was waged against the Cakchiquels after

they deserted Iximché, but it was not until early in 1525 when new reinforcements came from Mexico that Alvarado was finally able to defeat them. They always remained his enemies and in spirit were never conquered. Because of their hostility the Spaniards found it expedient to move their capital to a new site, still calling it Santiago.

Though there were rumors beginning even before the founding of the first capital that Alvarado was to be replaced by a King's favorite, this never happened. In 1526, leaving Guatemala in capable hands, Alvarado departed for Mexico to attend to some difficulties raised by his enemies. From Mexico he went to Spain, and it was there that the matter of governorship was settled once and for all. In 1527 by royal decree Alvarado was named Governor and Captain-General of Guatemala.

The colony at Zacaha was visited in 1690 by an early chronicler, Fray Francisco Vásquez. At that time descendants of Captain Cardona (and presumably of other settlers also) still lived there as small farmers. On this visit Vásquez saw the painting of the Virgin, known since the days of the Conquest as La Conquistadora. The memory of Fray Pontaza was still venerated by the inhabitants of the region.

The baby Leonor not only survived her campaigning but thrived on it and grew up into a young woman of great beauty. According to some historians, she married Puertocarrero at the age of thirteen. Later, in any event, she was the wife of Don Francisco de la Cueva, the brother of her Spanish stepmother Beatriz. By Cueva, Leonor had several children.

Doña Luisa died sometime before 1535 and Alvarado was killed in battle in June of 1541. In September of '41, an avalanche of water descending from the volcano Agua destroyed the third Spanish capital in Guatemala. It drowned the young Doña Beatriz, Alvarado's wife of three years, and all of his children known to be alive at that time, except Leonor.